BACK TOGETHER AGAIN

GRACIE YORK

Back Together Again

Jenni Bara and AJ Ranney writing as
GRACIE YORK

Back Together Again

Copyright @ 2024 Gracie York

All rights reserved.

No part of this book may be reproduced in any form or by any electric or mechanical means, including information storage and retrieval systems without prior written permission from the publisher.

The book is a work of fiction. The characters and events in this book are fictitious. Any similarity to real persons, living or dead, is purely coincidental and not intended by the author.

Line, Copy, Proofreading by Beth Lawton at VB Edits

Front cover art by Chelsea Kemp

Back cover art by Marvelous Dreams & Things

ISBN: 978-1-959389-18-7 (ebook)

ISBN: 978-1-959389-19-4 (paperback)

❦ Created with Vellum

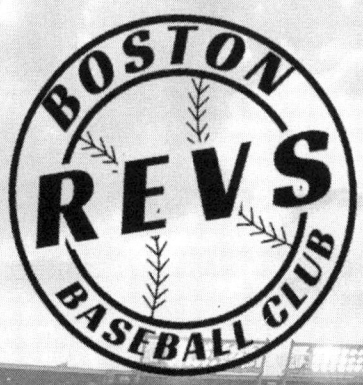

REVS | BANDITS
MAY 1ST | 6 PM

LINEUP

COACH: TOM WILSON #49

#	Player	Position
1	KYLE BOSCO #29	RF
2	JASEPER QUINN #16	1B
3	EMERSON KNIGHT #21	3B
4	ASHER PRICE #5	C
5	HENRY WINTERS #44	2B
6	EDDIE MARTINEZ #30	SS
7	COLTON STEWART #23	DH
8	TRISTIAN JENNER #27	LF
9	MASON DUMPTY #22	CF
P	CHRISTIAN DAMIANO #35	P

Playlist

Beautiful Mistakes - Maroon 5 & Megan Thee Stallion
Wolves - Selena Gomez
You Belong with Me - Taylor Swift
Something That I Want - Grace Potter
Home Run - Joe Nichols
Nothin' On You - B.O.B.
Slow Dancing in a Burning Room - John Mayer
Humpty Dumpty - AJR
Belong Together - Mark Ambor
Whatever it Takes - Imagine Dragons
The Night We Met - Lord Huron
Born to Love You - LANCO

For anyone waiting for the one who got away.

1

Mason

THE OVAL CRACKED between my teeth, releasing another burst of ranch. I swallowed the seed, then huffed a breath out, shooting the sunflower seed shell at my teammate.

Christian Damiano, our star pitcher, jumped up off the bench, swatting wildly at his arm where the shell hit. "What the fuck is wrong with you?"

"What's the matter? Afraid of a few germs, Dragon?" I teased the germophobe.

"Do you know how many strains of bacteria live in human salvia? It's disgusting." Damiano glared. He swore his nickname, Dragon, was because of his ability to throw the heat, but it had a whole lot more to do with his hostile personality. Only one person escaped his piss-poor moods.

"Funny how it's not an issue when it's *Avery*." I took every opportunity I could to razz him about his girlfriend. He had no issue with her drinking out of his cup or stealing his fork. Not to mention he was perfectly fine swapping saliva with her.

He lowered his chin a fraction, his jaw locking in a way that made his temple pulse. "Avery's perfect. She doesn't have germs."

"That's good, because she didn't wash her hands after she had Puff out earlier." Emerson Knight, our third baseman and Damiano's roommate, piped up. Puff was Avery's pet Northern Atlantic Puffin.

Damiano whipped his head around and set that glower on Emerson. "Puff is the cleanest bird ever."

The slight uncertainty that flitted across Damiano's face made me chuckle. The guy was so easy to mess with. Grumpy and paranoid made for the perfect combo.

"And she drank right out of the OJ bottle yesterday morning." Knight's smile was huge as he continued to taunt our pitcher.

"Stop fucking with me. You're all just jealous that I'm getting constant—" The words died on Damiano's tongue as he darted a look at our head coach, Tom Wilson. "That my girlfriend is perfect."

Wilson shook his head and snorted. "Sit the hell down and stop being an asshole, Damiano."

Those two had the weirdest relationship in the history of the Boston Revs. A year ago, they hated each other, but now, the relationship swung between coach, friend, and exasperated parent and his child. It made sense, though, since Avery was Coach Wilson's only child.

"I hate you both," he muttered as he dropped back onto the bench next to me. "Spit on me again, Humpty, and I swear I'll get Avery to put tiger shit in your locker."

"Always making Avery do your dirty work." Right fielder Kyle Bosco chuckled. As he leaned forward on the other side of Damiano, the stadium lights shone on the highlights in his hair. We'd all bet on whether they were natural, but he wouldn't confirm.

"She won't mind. Especially after I pay her back repeatedly with my tongue." He lifted his fist to Bosco.

Coach fisted his hands on his hips and snapped, "*Damiano.*"

The pitcher dropped his hand and winced.

"Love your daughter," he said, chin tipped high. "Like I said, she's perfect."

Wilson shook his head. "That's never what I question when it comes to your relationship with her."

All the guys within earshot laughed. Damn, I loved this team. And this was going to be our year.

The Revs owner and management had spent the last couple of years building a team that would finally bring home a world series title for Boston.

I'd had my doubts about the team three years ago when I was picked up as a free agent. I'd spent most of my life on the West Coast and wasn't all that excited about relocating to a cold-ass city like Boston. A city whose hockey team was dominating but who couldn't win a baseball game for shit.

I scanned the bench, taking in each of the guys. Now, though, I loved being here. And I wouldn't ever want to leave.

I couldn't even be upset when our shortstop went

down swinging, leaving a guy stranded on second because we were already leading three to one. We only needed three more outs to put yet another Revs win in the books. And we'd be that much closer to the top of the division.

Glove in hand, I headed out to center field. Boston Harbor was just beyond the wall behind me, and when the wind blew, it brought the smell of salt air with it. The light breeze cut the heat and humidity that could be more than a little oppressive in June. Its proximity to the water was one of the many reasons Lang Field—yes, the Langfields had really named this place *Lang Field*—was considered one of the best stadiums in the country.

Made sense that the Langfields would have the best. From my place at center field, I surveyed the owner's box. Like a king overlooking his kingdom, Beckett Langfield stood with his arms crossed over his chest, glaring down at the field. Just behind him, towering over him the way he towered over everyone, was Cortney Miller, the team's general manager. If the game was at Lang Field, both men would be here sporting their pinstripe Revs jerseys.

At the clap that echoed across the field of green, I snapped back into the moment, zeroing in on the plate. I didn't need to see the future to know that a ball was headed for the outfield wall. The telltale crack of the leather against wood said it all. With a man already on first base, this could be the go-ahead run.

Not going to happen.

I shifted, backpedaling, my eyes glued to the ball that was flying straight for center field. I turned and picked up my pace, running for the royal blue wall that separated Revs baseball from the rest of Boston. Kyle was headed my way from right, but I had this. I didn't need back up.

When the ball began to drop just a fraction, I knew I had a chance. I made it to the back wall just as the ball did. With my glove open to make the grab, I jumped up and flew. This was exactly the type of jump they paid me the big money to make. At the slight pressure at the tip of my glove, I forced my fingers shut, snapping the mitt tightly around the ball.

The crowd roared behind me as the stadium horns sounded.

My heart was soaring along with our fans, but before I could land and celebrate with the victory dance that had become my trademark, the spike of my cleat caught in the blue padding along the wall. Momentum and gravity pulled me, even as my foot was stuck three feet in the air.

I tipped, shoulders and head dropping fast. I had one second to make the choice. I could drop the ball and catch myself so I didn't smack headfirst into the dirt, or I could lock the ball up and save the out.

Who was I kidding? There was no choice. I'd never let my team down. Not with the game on the line. I locked my fingers tight in my glove and braced for the inevitable hard smack against the dirt.

"Shit, Humpty," Bosco called from a few feet away as he dove toward me.

It was too late. My head hit the ground, though the sensation barely registered before the world went black.

2

Rory

I can do this.

Not that I had a choice. I was the trainer assigned to treat neck and shoulder injuries. And our center fielder had just knocked himself out cold. The catch had been one for the books, but he was known for those plays—the ones ESPN would replay for weeks on end.

The three-and-a-half-foot jump to steal the home run away from the Bandits had been perfect.

Until it had gone horribly sideways.

Or, more accurately, upside down. Seconds after the ball had landed in his glove, the baseball star tipped. His foot had stayed halfway up the wall while the rest of his body headed fast and hard to the ground below.

The way his head bounced and tossed dirt around him would have made even the toughest of souls wince. He might be alert now, but he'd definitely be hurting by morning.

If it had been anyone else, I would have felt bad for the guy. Honestly, I almost felt bad for Mason Dumpty, and that was saying something. Since I'd started working for the Revs, I'd mostly avoided him. The few times we'd almost crossed paths I was able to dodge him, and I still wasn't sure if that left me angry with myself for being a wimp or relieved I didn't have to deal with him.

Maybe both.

I stepped up next to Kyle Bosco, the Revs' right fielder, and nodded to the team's doctor, letting him know I was here. Mason was sitting up, which was a whole lot better than dangling from his cleat. But his brows were pulled together as he scanned the not-so-small crowd that had gathered around him.

"You okay, Humpty?" Bosco asked.

Mason's frown deepened, creating a deep crease between his brows. "Am I Humpty Dumpty?"

Coach Wilson cocked his head to the side, and a few of the players chuckled. But Mason's expression remained confused as he looked past us to the field.

"The king's horses and all his men?" he slurred.

My stomach sank. He was talking nonsense, and that was *not* a good sign. I looked over my shoulder to see what he was talking about. The Revs mascots, dressed like soldiers on horseback, stood in their normal place along the sidelines. And Beckett Langfield was walking across the grass. When he approached, he pushed his way through the players and stood next to me. The Revs' GM, Cortney Miller, was right behind him.

"The king. We should kneel so the giant behind him doesn't take us out." Mason dropped his hands to the

BACK TOGETHER AGAIN

grass and pushed, trying to get up, but the doctor tightened his hold on his right arm and held him in place.

"Oh, for fuck's sake. He thinks Beckett's the king." Coach Wilson chuckled.

"Beckett thinks so too," Cortney muttered. But his expression was one of pure concern as he looked from the doctor to me and then back to Mason.

Mason blinked twice and rubbed his head.

With his hands on his hips, Cortney bent down. "How bad is it?"

Before I could answer, Mason turned to me. His jade green eyes were impossible to forget, even after eleven years. That single look sent a stream of memories whirling in my mind: the intensity flashing in his irises when he was working a puzzle, the spark when he laughed, the desire I thought I'd seen once upon a time.

My stomach flipped as a moment years ago took over. An instant when he pressed his full lips against mine.

Here, now, he ran his tongue over his lower lip and studied me, his gaze drifting from my eyes down to my mouth. The look sent a tingle rushing down my spine. Just like all those years ago, his attention lit me up from the inside out. I'd angled in a fraction before I realized what I was doing.

With a harsh breath in, I pulled back.

Dammit, I couldn't let him have this effect on me.

Not again.

Not after last time.

What the hell was wrong with me?

Mason Dumpty, known to his teammates as Humpty Dumpty—how the hell does a person earn a nickname like that?—was an asshole of epic proportion. Not to mention a member of the team I worked for and likely suffering from a serious concussion.

He should not be turning me on. I gritted my teeth and willed my body to get on board with my brain. Because no part of me liked the center fielder.

"Are you the princess?" Mason asked, focus still fixed on me.

"All right." Dr. Anderson cleared his throat and pushed to his feet. "He's done. We need to get him off the field."

"Done what?" Mason asked, searching the crowd around him again. "What's going on? Are we playing a game?" He dropped his chin, taking in his uniform and glove, and reached into his mitt. "Is this the game ball?"

Even after the fall, he'd miraculously held on to the ball. But that was Mason. He always made those shocking plays. The big saves when the game was on the line. The steal to second at the exact moment the team needed it. It would be a lie to say I hadn't followed his career over the years. He was an incredible ball player.

He held the baseball out to me. When no one stepped in to take it, I accepted it. The people around us were silent. Not one had answered his questions. Not the coach or the GM or the owner of the team. Probably because he wouldn't remember this tomorrow. Hell, he probably wouldn't remember this in ten minutes.

I crouched next to him and sighed. "You hit your head and need to get checked out."

Confusion swam in his eyes as he assessed me. "You'll come?"

"I'll ride along," Dr. Anderson said, pulling out his phone and tapping the screen rapidly, probably getting the ambulance ready.

Coach Wilson waved a hand to the ground crew to bring out the cart.

"Should we be worried?" Beckett asked behind me as Mason continued to stare at me.

"Of course we should," Cortney said.

Mason finally looked away from me and focused on the blond giant.

"His brain is probably bleeding, or he might have cracked his skull. He'll need a CT with contrast, an MRI of his neck and shoulders…"

Mason's eyes got wider and wider as Cortney went on.

"Let's not panic yet," I said, cutting the spiral of thoughts known to come from our general manager. It would only make matters worse if the GM sent Mason into panic mode too.

"Let's not say too much until we have some firm answers," Dr. Anderson agreed as the cart rolled to a stop and the rest of the team stepped back.

"Yeah, don't panic." Beckett, arms crossed over his chest, glared at his GM.

"Let's get the game going again. And you two." Dr. Anderson waved at the owner and the GM. "Go deal with the press. The last thing we want is them chasing the ambulance for a statement. Get the PR team to put something out there like 'heading to hospital. Condition stable but unknown.'"

Chuckles echoed around me. Stable? That remained to be seen, but unknown seemed to fit.

"Are we going to the castle now?" Mason asked. "Is this a chariot?" He homed in on the glorified golf cart we'd use to get him off the field.

"Yep, sure is." I nodded and shot him a pacifying smile as I stood up so the guys could move Mason onto the back of the cart.

Two men helped him to his feet and kept him steady. All the while, he was watching me, his brows pinched. With a wince, he grabbed for his head and swayed, forcing the men to hold on a bit tighter.

Beckett pointed at me. "You go with him."

"Me?" What could I do for extreme confusion caused by a concussion? Yes, I said we shouldn't panic, and I meant it, but he probably would need a CT and full workup of his head.

Beckett narrowed his eyes at me. "Yeah, you're neck and shoulders. You should be there to work on the treatment plan. The way he's cradling that left arm makes me think his head isn't the only thing that needs to be addressed."

He didn't even wait for me to respond before turning to Cortney. "Once we deal with the press, we'll meet them at the hospital."

Great. That meant there was no escape for me.

3

Mason

Slowly, I forced my eyelids open, but the piercing light that immediately assaulted me had me snapping them shut again. The groan I let out was met by the sound of curtains being pulled shut. I tried the simple task once more, this time finding myself in a dimly lit room.

My general manager's face came into view as I scanned my surroundings. High ceilings, hardwood floors, a stone fireplace, and thick molding. The place was old, probably built in the 1800s, but it had been restored to twenty-first-century perfection.

"Where am I?" I sat up on the oversized tan sectional, fighting a wave of dizziness as I did.

Cortney towered over me, crossing his arms over his Revs T-shirt. "My house."

"Why?" A year ago, it wouldn't have been weird to sleep on his couch. But a year ago, he was the team's catcher. He had retired at the end of last season so he could spend more time with his pregnant fiancée. And because he was smart as hell and knew every stat for every player in the league, the Langfields had hired him and put him in the role of general manager. Technically, he was my super boss and could easily cut or trade me.

He sighed. "Your family's across the country, and we couldn't send you back to your apartment alone."

Rubbing my aching head, I raised one brow at him. Because I couldn't be alone, his first thought was to bring me to his house?

"Don't look at me like that. I was at the hospital with you for hours." His blond man bun bobbed as he shook his head. "I might be stuck in a suit most days, but I'm still the guy who wears shamrock socks to every game."

When the memory of the day Cortney thought he'd lost his lucky socks floated into my mind, I couldn't help but smile. That moment of panic for him was what led him to Dylan. But I hadn't realized he still wore them so religiously. "Seriously?"

He shrugged. "Yep. They're lucky."

I chuckled and shook my head, but the moment I did, I wished I hadn't. Even the slight moment sent pain shooting between my temples. Wincing, I closed my eyes. Cortney was talking about the doctor, physical therapy, waking every three hours, and what I thought was a comment about not staying by myself. I was trying to keep up, but I was finding it hard to grasp what he was saying.

"And don't forget the sling for your arm." He nodded at the square coffee table in front of me.

I frowned at the blue and white piece of fabric. "Seriously? My shoulder feels—" I lifted it and rolled, but instantly regretted it when another shot of pain hit me.

"Yeah, not great," Cortney finished.

I slumped back, shutting my eyes again.

"Hey, Mason, you're riding with me to the stadium," a familiar female voice said.

I cracked one eye open, finding Cortney's fiancée, Dylan, standing in the middle of the room, holding their baby girl.

"I have to be there at nine, and you're meeting with Rory and the team doctor."

Rory? Hmm. Rory, Rory. Nope. The name didn't ring a bell.

Cortney sidled up beside Dylan and took the baby who had a full head of strawberry blond hair. She rested her cheek on her daddy's massive shoulder as he rubbed her back. "I don't know why I still have to ride with Beckett every day."

Dylan's laugh lit up the room so bright I had to close my eyes once again. "It's just what the universe wants."

"No. It's what Beckett wants."

Cortney and Beckett spent practically every waking minute together. Their wives were best friends, and their families lived in side-by-side brownstones. On top of all that, they worked together and carpooled to the office. I'd always assumed they got along, even if they bickered like an old married couple.

"Eh." With a shrug, she lifted onto her toes and kissed him on the side of his neck. "You humor him because you love me. And we both love that he's letting us open a branch of Little Fingers at Lang Field so Willow can be near you all day." She dropped back down and turned to me. "Grab sunglasses. It's bright out."

Then she was gone, spinning on her bare feet and bouncing out of the room, all red curls and flowing white dress.

Cortney watched her the entire way, and when he turned back to me, he was sporting the kind of sappy smile that belonged to a guy in love.

I didn't want to say I was jealous, but at twenty-nine, I was starting to realize I might be ready for something like what my former teammate had found.

Maybe not kids yet, but someone I could look at the way Cortney looked at his fiancée.

"You okay?" he asked as his daughter yanked on his blond man bun.

"Yeah," I muttered, even as I rested my head back on the sofa and closed my eyes. The conversation alone had left me exhausted.

It didn't compare to the level of exhaustion that overtook me twenty minutes later as I rode to the stadium with Dylan. The sling was uncomfortable, especially once I was strapped into the seat belt. The sunglasses were pointless, even inside the SUV with tinted windows. Currently, the light wasn't what was causing my head to pound. No, it was the two women up front and five loud-as-shit little people in the back seat. The baby girl had been crying on and off since Cortney had clicked her car seat in, and two of the other kids were fighting about who could spy more red things.

"You shouldn't sleep, Mr...." a girl's voice called out, although I had no idea how she thought I could sleep.

"Mr. Dumpty, Collette," Liv Langfield, Beckett's wife, answered.

"Huh. Statistically, what are the chances that a man named Dumpty fell off a wall and broke his head?" another girl asked.

"Probably a lot, because he does the tricks," a young boy answered.

A Nerf bullet bounced off my ear.

"Fuck's sake," I muttered.

"Umm, excuse me—"

"No, Phoebe." Dylan cut her off. "Bill Uncle Cortney."

"Yeah, or Uncle Beckett. We won't charge the invalid," Liv added.

Charge? What the hell? I rubbed my head.

If Cortney and Beckett had also headed to the stadium, then why was I in the circus car with five kids?

"Finn, Addy, Collette, Phoebe, remember: we need to use quiet voices because Mason has a concussion," Dylan said, her voice tranquil yet cheery.

"Why didn't Cortney and Beckett take him along with them?" Liv voiced what I had been asking myself since we left.

"Oh, you know Beckett. He doesn't leave until eight thirty, and if Mason had waited around for them, then he wouldn't have made it in time."

The crying baby finally quieted, easing the pounding in my head a fraction. I let out a long breath and shut my eyes. I wished they would stop talking too, but telling the wives of the owner and the GM to shut up would not make me any friends in the office.

"I could have convinced Beckett to leave earlier."

"Then that blackness that sometimes tinges his aura would have settled over him, and that would have stressed Cort out. If that happened, then all that negative energy would have been bad for Mason's brain bleed."

Before I could even fully understand what Dylan had just said, another Nerf bullet ricocheted off my head.

What the hell?

"Finn, he has a head injury. Let's not shoot the guy with the bleeding brain," Liv scolded her son.

Hold up. Maybe I needed to pay more attention to my head injury.

"Do I really have a brain bleed?"

"It's just a moderate concussion," the driver answered. "You'll be out for about ten days. At least that's the rumor."

My head throbbed, partially because I'd be out for *ten* days, but also because the baby was crying again.

It seemed strange that no one had filled me in on what was wrong with my head. Or maybe they had, and I couldn't remember. Cortney had mentioned a few things this morning, but when I reached for those memories, my brain was fuzzy. The last thing I remembered before I woke up on his couch was sitting on the bench and fucking around with the guys. Maybe I did have a brain bleed. But if that were the case, wouldn't they keep me in the hospital? I told myself I'd ask the team doc this morning.

Except by the time I was sitting in front of him, my brain was a jumbled mess again, and I couldn't remember what I wanted to ask.

"Beckett will be here in a minute," Cortney

announced as he stepped into the exam room and shut the door behind him. "He's trying to get confirmation that we'll have Potters called up by tomorrow."

I nodded.

But why was he in here?

Heck, why was I in here? I had been trying hard to pay attention to what the doc was saying, but I was too focused on the trainer he'd introduced as Rory. Because Rory hadn't stopped glaring at me since the doc asked if I remembered her. She seemed familiar, but I couldn't place how. I'd never seen her around the stadium, I don't think, but apparently, she had been out on the field with me when I came to.

Like I said, the last twelve hours were really fuzzy.

"You can't be alone. Not for the next few days. Maybe longer," Doc said as Beckett stepped into the room, wearing his signature scowl.

The words registered. Was he shitting me? So I'd be stuck with a babysitter for the foreseeable future?

"You can come back to my house." Cortney took a step to the side as Beckett stepped up next to him.

Nope. That was not happening. I shook my head and was instantly hit with a stabbing pain in my temples. Shit. Grasping my head, I ducked and squeezed my eyes shut.

"No offense, but with all the shit going on in your house, it registered somewhere between a circus and an insane asylum."

"Dude—" Cortney started.

"He's not wrong." Beckett smirked.

"The car ride alone left my head pounding." I glanced

up at Beckett. "I doubt your house is any better since half the people in the car live with you."

"Good thing I'm not offering, then." Beckett's scowl was back.

"I'll stay with one of the guys." I shrugged. Neither Emerson nor Bosco would mind. Even Damiano would let me hang with him and Avery.

Beckett roughed a hand down his face. "We're all about to get on a plane, remember?"

"What? Why?" I blinked, searching my memory for plans I'd made to leave Boston. Was I going back to California to see my parents?

Beckett cocked his head to the side, and Cortney let out a loud sigh.

What was I forgetting?

When it finally dawned on me, my stomach sank. "We have a six-day road stretch."

They nodded in unison.

I lifted one shoulder. Even if I wasn't cleared to play, I could still tag along, right? "I'll just go with the team."

Beckett narrowed his eyes and lowered his chin. "You're not flying on day one of a concussion."

"Correct. The pressure changes could have negative effects on the swelling," Dr. Anderson agreed.

"Then what do you suggest I do?"

"Issues like this are one of the many reasons we have training staff." Beckett turned to Rory. "You're neck and shoulders, right? He can stay with you."

Her eyes widened, and her face went pale. For an instant, her attention snapped to me, but then she turned back to Beckett. "I—um…"

"You have to rehab his shoulder anyway. It makes sense."

Her mouth fell open, but that initial look of shock quickly morphed into one that screamed *pissed off*. What the hell had I done to this woman to warrant her animosity? Had I said something offensive in my stupor last night?

I assessed her again. Gorgeous tits, full hips. That hourglass shape that always drew my eye. Maybe I hit on her. Shit. Pretty eyes, pouty lips. She looked vaguely familiar, but my mind couldn't make the connection. I hadn't spent much time with the training staff since I'd played for the Revs, and she was new this year.

All the thinking and trying to connect the dots made my head throb again.

Closing my eyes and letting my shoulders slump, I rubbed at my forehead, willing the ache to dull. Damn, I was tired.

"I'm not guaranteeing ten days."

Dr. Anderson's words brought me back to the conversation. I lifted my head and focused on him again.

"Heads are funny sometimes. It can take longer to put them back together again."

"Right." Beckett gave a clipped nod. "So it makes sense for him to stay with Miss Humphreys while the team travels this week."

The second the name left his lips, images flashed through my mind, and everything clicked together.

Humphreys. That was why she seemed so familiar. And furious.

Aurora Humphreys had hated me since high school.

4

Rory

IT TOOK everything in me to keep my composure.

One of the reasons I'd wanted to work for Boston's hockey team—*not* their baseball team—was because I wanted nothing to do with Mason Dumpty. I had applied to be a trainer for the Boston Bolts, but the Revs had offered me the job. For an instant, I'd considered turning it down, but I would have been an idiot if I did. This job was highly sought after. And with any luck, when a position opened up with the Bolts, I could transfer. But for now, I was stuck with the asshole who *still* didn't remember me.

And why would he? I wasn't anything special to him. I was the one who'd crushed on him in high school while he'd kept me firmly in the friend zone. Except for that one night. I'd been a silly little girl back then, head over heels for a boy who barely noticed me. But never again would I fall for those green eyes and perfect smile.

In the years since high school, I'd fortified my walls. There was no way a man like him could break through them. But that didn't mean I wanted to be stuck with the jerk for the entire week.

I slammed the car into park, and a second later, Cortney opened the passenger door. He bent his six-foot-six frame almost in half, and his face came into view.

"You sure you're good with this?"

If I said no, he'd find another solution without argument. All I had to do was play the *I'm a female* card, and this would all go away. But I was a female in a male dominated industry. It had taken hard work and dedication to get here, and if I couldn't do all that was asked of me, there was a line of people a mile long waiting to take my place.

Cortney raised a brow and regarded me with a genuinely empathetic expression. "Langfield can be a bossy ass, but if you don't want to do this, we can ask someone else."

I glanced over at Mason and Beckett, who were arguing with one another while Beckett pulled a duffel bag out of the back of a large SUV parked a few spots over.

Though my stomach twisted, I sighed and let my shoulders drop. "No, it's fine."

For years, I'd dreamed of landing a job as a trainer with a professional sports team. Now that I was here, doing what I loved, I refused to blow it over some old high school crush.

"Okay. But if you have any problems, just call me."

Cortney shuffled back and stood to his full height.

"Pop the trunk," Beckett demanded as he approached. Once he'd tossed the bag inside, he slammed the trunk and gave it a pat. Then he stepped up beside Cortney on the sidewalk.

Mason eyed me warily as he slowly climbed in and shut the door. "I'm perfectly fine to stay by myself."

I rolled my eyes as I headed for the road. "Nope. The last thing I want to do is lose my job because the center fielder died of a brain bleed on my watch."

He huffed and rubbed his head. "The doctor said there was no bleeding, but it's confusing as heck when everyone else keeps tossing that around."

His Adam's apple bobbed as he swallowed hard. At the sight of the uncertainty written all over his face, I was swamped with remorse. With his concussion, he was probably struggling with confusion.

"Do you have a guest room?" he asked before I could apologize. He shifted and pulled on the sling cradling his arm like it was offensive rather than protecting his sore shoulder.

Giving him a load of side-eye, I raised my eyebrow.

"Just wondering if I'm going to be stuck on a too-small couch."

"You can have my bed. I'll take the couch."

"I have a guest room." Now his eyes were closed and he was resting his head against the seat. "We could stay at my place."

My initial instinct was to shout "hell no." But after a moment of thought, it made sense. His apartment had to be bigger than my one-bedroom. And that meant it would be easier to keep more distance between us. "I need to stop and get my stuff."

His only response was a nod. For the next fifteen minutes, silence reigned. Which was fine by me.

Once I'd parked, I unbuckled and grabbed the door handle.

"I can wait in the car."

I froze with the door ajar. "Yeah, no. As long as you're my responsibility, I'm not letting you out of my sight. Even though your brain isn't currently bleeding, the possibility that it could is why everyone is worried."

He narrowed his eyes, but only for an instant before he winced and pain flashed across his face again.

"Okay." He sighed, rubbing at his temple.

After putting together a small bag, I made my way back to where I'd left Mason in my living room. He was standing near an end table, holding a photo.

I stopped in my tracks when I realized it was one of me from high school. Shit. Had he put two and two together?

He looked up, and I swore there was a hint of a smile curling his lips. "You were always hot as a brunette, but I like the blond look too."

I ran my hand through the ends of my highlighted hair. Yeah, it was a good five shades lighter than my natural color. "It took seeing an old picture to finally remember me?" I crossed my arms and sighed.

"I knew who you were before we left the office." He smirked. "It's ironic that you blew me off eleven years ago, but now you're stuck with me."

I *blew* him *off? Was he kidding me?*

5

Mason

I shook my head as I stared at the photo in my hands. How had I not seen her in the weeks she'd been working at Lang Field? Eighteen-year-old me had been obsessed with her. She was the smartest girl in school, and she never put up with anyone's shit. Including mine.

By some miracle, she and I had been paired up as lab partners during my senior year. She was a grade behind me, but even then, her sinful curves were all woman. Add in a dimpled smile and long lashes that she hid behind those thick black glasses, and she was the star of all my teenage fantasies.

Near the end of the school year, I had all but begged her to come to one of my teammate's parties. We had been flirting for months, and I thought maybe I'd get to spend my last summer before college getting to call the bombshell of a girl mine.

Boy, had I been wrong.

"You talked me into coming to the party that I wasn't even invited to." She crossed her arms over her chest, taking a defensive stance. "You kissed me, and then you disappeared into a bedroom with another girl." Her jaw tightened. "In no world was that *me* blowing *you* off."

My heart and my stomach both plummeted. Was that what she'd been thinking for all these years? That I just left her for another girl?

"You remember what happened to Ian that night, right?"

"Who?" Frowning, she tilted her head, causing her ponytail to brush over the shoulder of her blue shirt.

I was instantly captivated by the way the blond strands rested over the swell of her tits. The fabric of the Revs polo pulled taut across her chest, and the two buttons she'd done up strained enough to make them look like they'd pop open with the slightest help.

She cleared her throat, and my eyes snapped up to her face.

What were we talking about?

I blinked, willing my mind to focus on the conversation. With a deep breath in, I tore my attention away from her and scanned the room. I didn't recognize the place. Which made sense, because I was in Aurora's apartment. Shit. I had to get my head in the game. The fog that hovered in my mind was frustrating enough to have me clenching my jaw, which only made my head hurt worse.

Her apartment was very her. Cute but totally uncluttered. From the look of things, she liked the girlie shit—curtains and plants and stupid knickknacks that collected dust—but nothing was out of place. The full wall of bookshelves sent warmth unfurling in my chest and made me smile. Eleven years ago, my girl had always had a book in her backpack. Quite a few of my own favorites held key spots on her shelf. Not many of my friends realized I was a super reader, especially back then. It didn't go with the shit-stirring jock image I'd cultivated. But Aurora knew me better than most people. At least she used to.

"Mason?"

At the sound of my name, I blinked at her, my brain clouding once again. What had we been saying?

She frowned again, concern swimming in her irises. "Ian?"

Right, I was talking about my best friend from high school. I almost shook my head to clear the cobwebs but stopped myself when I remembered that it hurt like hell to do it. I pulled out my phone and opened the most recent picture of my best friend. It was from last Christmas. He and his wife stood behind their three kids, both wearing big smiles.

When I turned the screen toward her, she studied the photo, but there wasn't a hint of recognition in her gaze.

"Ian Tilton?"

"Oh." She focused on me again, pressing her teeth into her bottom lip. "You played baseball together, right? He played second base?"

"Yeah," I said. "My best friend."

She pursed her lips and regarded me for another moment. "I vaguely remember him, I guess..."

Maybe she did, but the puzzle pieces still weren't clicking for her.

"He ODed that night. Remember that?"

"I, umm." She shook her head. "When people started yelling about the cops coming and taking off, I left too. Didn't everyone leave?"

"I didn't. I stayed. With the police and the paramedics." I was more concerned about Ian than I was about the consequences that could have come from being caught there. "Ian passed out in one of the bedrooms upstairs, so his girlfriend Kristy came to the backyard looking for me. She couldn't get him to wake up. I'm the one who called 911. And that's when everyone ran."

Her eyes widened, and she put a hand to her mouth. "All I heard after that night was that the cops broke up the party and a couple of people got in trouble."

I huffed. "Ian was the mayor's kid, so the details got buried. His dad made sure of it." I pinned her with my stare, because after eleven years, I had questions too. "But I texted you, so many times, and you never responded."

"I panicked. I was terrified. My parents would have killed me if they knew I was there. When that girl came out and whispered in your ear, you followed her without a glance back at me. So I followed you. And I saw you go into the bedroom with her." She blinked rapidly, as if fighting off tears. As if the memory still upset her.

Shit. Knowing she was hurt made my chest ache. But

why the fuck would she think I would leave her for some other girl?

She cleared her throat. "I was devastated. So I blocked you before I even got home that night."

"You never got any of my texts?" I shook my head and immediately regretted it. Another pricking pain raced through my skull. This one was sharp enough to have me dropping onto her couch and putting my head down in my hands.

"Mason, we don't have to talk about this."

"No, I want to." Those first few weeks of June had sucked. My best friend had almost died. Then he'd been moved to rehab, and I couldn't contact him. And at the same time, the girl I was obsessed with wouldn't talk to me.

"Don't stress yourself." She placed her hand on my good shoulder and gave it a light squeeze.

The warmth of her palm bled through my thin T-shirt. I swallowed hard, fighting the rush that worked through my body at her touch. I wanted more of it. I craved it.

Before I could get my fill, she pulled back and frowned down at me. "We don't have to talk about this. Not right now. Let's go back to your apartment and talk over lunch. We have days, remember?"

I watched her, calling up an image of her as a sixteen-year-old. The girl with dark hair and glasses that I was obsessed with for well over a year. It's insane that I didn't recognize her right away or even that I hadn't seen her in the few weeks she'd been working with the team.

Did I really pay that little attention to the staff around

the stadium? Maybe I did. My head throbbed, and my thoughts drifted back to years ago. What really happened after that night? It was all a blur. I wished, more than anything, that I could focus on it, understand how the events had played out. But she was right. We had plenty of time to hash out the details.

6

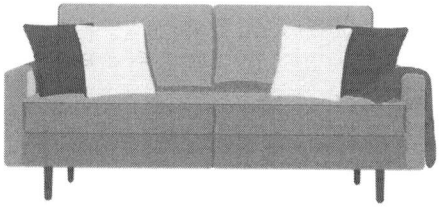

Rory

THOUGH I SHOULDN'T HAVE BEEN SURPRISED by the sight in front of me, my breath caught and my eyes went wide. It made sense that Mason would live in a fancy high-rise apartment, but the extravagance of the full glass building, the waterfall feature out front, and garden circle with valet was intimidating. I almost wished I'd insisted on staying at my rinky-dink place.

Before I'd even come to a stop in the circle in front of the entrance, Mason was pushing open the door and hopping out. I rolled the window down and sucked in a breath, ready to call his name, because I had no idea what to do from here, and he'd just left me without instructions.

But he just strutted away like he wasn't suffering from a concussion. "Hey, man." Mason spun his sling away from the man standing by the front doors like he was trying to hide the injury and slapped palms with him.

"Dude, that catch was some shit."

Mason chuckled and, in his sling and everything, tucked his arm into his chest and bounced his shoulders, doing the dance that fans loved. "Gotta make the big plays. Can't say I remember it, though."

The guy shook his head. "I wouldn't watch it if I were you."

"If only I'd stuck the landing," Mason joked, waggling his brows.

The guy chuckled. "You out for a while?"

Mason's smile stayed plastered to his face, but the light flickered from his eyes. "Depends on what they can do to put my head back together. It's all foggy, man."

"Sucks."

"This is my shadow for the next few days," Mason said, pointing my way. "Can we find a place for her car? Just put it on my tab."

"Absolutely."

As the guy headed my way, I climbed out of the car and opened the back door so I could get my bag. When I straightened again, the man was beside me, hauling it out of my arms. "We'll send that up, ma'am."

"Oh." I blinked and stepped back. "Right. Sorry."

Once he'd confirmed that I'd left the keys in the car and that all I needed was the one bag, Mason waved me over.

The second we were in the elevator, he let his smile fall. His eyelids drooped, too, as he rubbed his temples.

"You okay?"

He opened his eyes and examined me for a beat. "I don't know."

The honesty in the answer yanked at my chest. He'd been in good spirits all day, or he'd at least put on an impressive act, but it was obvious that he was hurting.

"It's rough keeping up conversations. Hell, it's hard to remember where I am, even if I *know*, you know?" His eyes went wide, and he waved a hand like he was afraid I would panic. "It's just"—he frowned—"confusing for a second or two."

I rubbed his good arm, going for soothing. "It will get back to normal, but healing takes time. For head injuries especially."

He lowered his chin, fixating on where my palm was still splayed over his warm skin. I pulled it back quickly.

"Will it?" He swallowed and rested his head against the stainless-steel wall. "Because I like how it used to be, and I miss that."

The words were mumbled and far off, like he was talking about more than just the concussion. When the elevator dinged, he finally opened his eyes. He ushered me out into the hallway, then toward one of the two doors on this floor. Inside his apartment, I was met with a massive open-concept living space and an incredible view of the city.

"Wow." I had to fight back the tingles working their way through me as I took in the Boston skyline. This was so out of my league.

"Yeah, I thought it was weird."

Weird was the last word I'd use to describe this place. It was gorgeous, stunning. Expensive.

"Who would have thought we'd have the exact same sofa?"

What?

I spun away from the window, and sure enough, a sofa identical to the one I'd bought at Ashley Furniture sat in the middle of his living room. Along with the couch, he had the chair and love seat to complete the set.

For a moment, I continued taking in his space and discovered a larger version of my table.

"Table too," I mumbled.

"There's that expression about minds." He frowned, his emerald irises going dull. "Like they all think good."

I bit back a chuckle. The poor guy was struggling, and the last thing I wanted to do was make him feel worse.

"Great minds think alike."

He snapped his fingers and pointed at me. "Yes. That's why we always liked the same music and TV shows."

He was right. We'd discovered so many commonalities during those months that we'd been lab partners. He had been more into sports than I was, but otherwise, we enjoyed so many of the same things. Even though he was the typical popular jock and I was anything but, we'd connected over our love of science and music.

He would come over to work on homework, and we would talk and laugh for hours. If we hadn't existed in completely different social circles, maybe we would have become more. Maybe something would have happened before that night he kissed me. But every time we were together around other kids from school, his friends always seemed to pull him away.

Each time, I'd remember that I wasn't good enough

for him. His friends knew it too. And that night, when the girl had pulled him away from me, in my mind, hadn't been an exception. It was just one more instance of someone from his friend group saving him from the pathetic nerd who looked at him with hearts in her eyes.

For one second, I wondered how different it would have been if I hadn't blocked him so quickly. If I'd gone to see him after my mom told me he stopped by the house. If I'd given him a chance to explain.

"Finishing *Bones* wasn't the same without you around."

I blinked back to the present and ducked my chin. "I didn't finish it."

"Really?" He cocked his head. "Why?"

I'd never admit that it hurt to watch it without him, so I summoned my best look of indifference and said, "No time."

"Hmm." He looked at me for a long minute, almost as if he could see there was more to the story. But then a bolt of confusion flashed in his green irises, and once again, he'd lost track of the conversation.

I let out a sigh of relief. It wasn't one we needed to have anyway.

"What do you want to do for lunch?" I changed topics.

He dropped onto the sofa and slumped back, closing his eyes. "We ordering something? I'd love to say I'm an amazing cook, but I'm not, so what are we doing?" The last sentence came out mumbled, like he was exhausted.

I glanced around, taking in the books on his shelves. Our tastes were similar in that respect too. From what I could see, I had more romance than he did, but he had plenty of books.

"How about we order pizza, and I can read *The Sorcerer's Stone* to you?" With a concussion, watching TV was out, and in high school, we'd both loved Harry Potter, so hopefully he didn't think it was a stupid suggestion.

He smiled. "When you read it to me the last time, you used all kinds of voices."

My cheeks heated, so I dropped my chin to hide the blush. *God, I was such a dork in high school.* "I was just messing around."

"I thought you did a good job." With his eyes still closed, he pointed toward the kitchen. "The takeout menus are in the closest drawer to the fridge. The one for the pizza place around the corner should be on top. You still a ham and pineapple fan?"

"Yup. Still my favorite." I pushed to my feet and pulled open the drawer.

"Mine too. Get that."

Once I'd ordered, I wandered back into the living area, my palms sweaty and my heart beating a little too quickly. I wasn't sure what to do next, and I wasn't sure how to be alone with this man.

He hummed from his spot on the couch, sending a tiny wave of comfort through me. "You should read the illustrated one by Jim Kay. You'll love it."

Mason still hadn't opened his eyes or moved from where he'd planted himself when we arrived. I wouldn't be surprised if he was fast asleep by the time the pizza came.

I moved over toward the shelves anyway.

"Middle one, second shelf from the bottom."

Sure enough, the large illustrated editions of the first five Harry Potter books were there.

I hadn't gotten them yet, although I'd eyed them more than once. I already had two sets of the books, and I really didn't have the space for a third. Mason clearly didn't have that issue. His bookshelves covered one entire wall of his massive apartment. But he'd been drafted straight to the Revs after his senior year at Penn State, so he was in his eighth season with the team, and he was making eight figures a year.

I crouched and pulled the book from the shelf, then shuffled to the chair.

A few pages in, we were both lost in the Potterverse. It was amazing how the story could grip me and make time fly, no matter how many times I'd read it. I had strong-armed Mason into reading the series during Christmas break of his senior year. He'd teased me endlessly about how it had ruined his week because he couldn't put the books down.

Once the pizza arrived and I'd plated a couple of slices for each of us, we continued reading. I'd just finished a second slice when movement from Mason drew my eye again. More than once, he'd lifted his left arm and winced. Although nothing was torn and his shoulder wouldn't require surgery, the impact had caused some swelling in his rotator cuff.

"We probably need to do some exercises." I closed the book and stood up.

Ignoring his sigh of annoyance, I helped him remove his shirt and get situated in a chair, then stood in front of him. I settled so that one of my legs was on each side of his thick thighs.

Clearing his throat, he shifted in the chair. The movement made the outer edge of his gray sweats brush against my inner thighs. He froze, his attention fixed on my black pants, and swallowed harshly. A tension buzzed in the air between us, sending my pulse skyrocketing and making my breaths come faster.

He fisted his hands on his legs and grimaced, almost like he was in pain, but I hadn't even touched his shoulder. This stretch was common. It was one I did with players almost daily. Not once had it felt weird. And yet, right now, I was half ready to jump out of my skin and half wanting to lean closer to him.

But this was my job. *Get a grip, Rory.* Giving myself a mental lecture, I let out a breath. Then I gripped his left wrist and slowly guided it across his body.

As we stretched his muscles, his intense jade eyes locked on me. My palms on his warm bare skin made my stomach tighten. He studied my face and paused for a heartbeat on my lips before focusing on my eyes. My heart pounded in my chest. And for a second, I forgot to breathe. I couldn't look away, not even if I wanted to. And I definitely didn't want to.

"You know I would have never blown you off, right?" His words were laced with a fierce desperation. Like he needed me to believe him. "Not then, and not now."

I searched his face for any indication that he was lying. As much as I wanted that to be the truth, the awkward girl buried deep inside me wasn't sure that something wouldn't get in our way again.

7

Mason

SHE WAS SO CLOSE. Maybe six inches from me. But that gap was shrinking bit by bit, like an invisible string was tugging us closer. I could snake my arm around her waist and have her settled on my lap before she knew what was happening. Or maybe she already understood my thoughts. If the hitch in her breath and the way her eyes were dilated were any indication, then that was the case.

Before I could act on it, though, she stepped back. As the warmth that had surrounded me vanished, disappointment crashed over me in a tidal wave.

Why did she have such a profound effect on me? Before I could process that thought, the stark white circle that surrounded the Revs logo on her shirt captured my attention, reminding me without words that we couldn't cross that line. She'd always wanted this career. Even when she was a junior in high school, back when I was still drifting aimlessly, without a clue about what I wanted, she knew. She'd talked about her dream of one day working for a professional team. Hockey was her first choice, but she hadn't minded the idea of working for a pro baseball team either. While she had her sights set on her future, all I wanted was her.

Pain lanced through my shoulder, pulling me from my trance and making me wince.

She backed up another step, then another. "You need to ice. I'll get something."

Nodding, I dragged myself back to the sofa. Once I was flat on my back, I tucked my good arm behind my head. "There's a bag of peas in freezer."

I forced my body to relax, breathing through the pain in my shoulder and the dull throb in my head, and tracked Aurora as she moved across the apartment. And fuck if I wasn't an asshole. Because when she bent over the freezer, giving me the perfect view of her ass, I couldn't help but smirk. She wasn't tiny, and that was perfect. I had big hands, and from here, it was easy to see that my palms would fit perfectly molded around the globes of her ass. Before I'd had my fill, she stood up and spun around. Looked like I'd have to bury the bag of peas better next time.

In less than a minute, she had the peas on my shoulder and was collecting the plates we'd used for pizza and bustling around the kitchen.

My eyes drifted shut, the exhaustion of the day weighing on me. When I opened them again, she was curled up on the love seat, wearing her dark-framed glasses, attention locked in on her book. *Iron Flame*. Interesting.

"I read that one when it came out." My voice was gruff from sleep. As I pulled the bag of peas from my shoulder, I cleared my throat.

"Really?" She lifted her head and scanned my bookshelves like she was searching for it.

"I spend so much time on the plane, so I read on my phone a lot. I only buy physical copies of my favorites."

"So this series didn't earn a place?" She lifted one brow in challenge. Hmm. She must have loved them so far.

"I'll see when the series is done. I won't buy a set until it's full."

With a smile, she nodded. "I remember that about you. You were horrified when I bought *Cinder* and *Scarlett* before we knew whether we actually liked the series."

"Turned out you were right. It was epic."

She flashed a smile, and my stomach bottomed out. Behind the glasses she was sporting—she must have taken her contacts out at some point—her brown eyes sparkled.

God, how had I ever forgotten the feeling I got when she smiled at me? I gave my teammate Dragon so much shit for how willing he was to turn himself into a pretzel if it made his girl happy, but as I sat here, soaking in the warmth that hit me when Aurora smiled at me, it was easy to remember how easily I'd become that guy eleven years ago and how easily I could fall right back into that role.

My stomach rumbled loudly.

"Someone's hungry."

I rested a hand on my abdomen. "Growing boys need their food."

She chuckled and shook her head. "That might have worked at eighteen, but you're twenty-nine. You're done growing."

Surprised by my hunger since I'd put away a few slices of pizza, I glanced at the clock. "Oh shit, it's almost seven."

"Yeah, you were out for a while, Sleeping Beauty," she teased.

With a chuckle, I pushed to my feet and headed for the kitchen. I wanted to figure out dinner before the game came on, so I pulled open the fridge and surveyed the meals Jeanie had left.

"Is this okay for dinner?" I asked, setting what looked to be a chicken and broccoli pasta on the marble countertop.

She stepped up next to me at the island. "I thought you didn't cook."

"I don't." I shrugged. "I have someone who drops off food and cleans."

"Every day?"

"Not when I'm away." I turned and preheated the oven.

At first, I had tried to do it all myself. My family didn't have a ton of money when I was growing up, and I felt more comfortable cleaning and cooking—or ordering takeout—myself. But during my first season with the Revs, I learned that paying someone to do things here and there made my life infinitely less complicated. I wasn't wasteful. I respected that my time was just as valuable to me as money.

"But I'm at the stadium most days until eight or nine o'clock, so I don't have time to do this stuff."

"I guess that makes sense." She shrugged.

"She cooks and cleans, even does my laundry. It means when I come home, I have time to relax. And I need that."

"Because every minute you're outside these walls, you have to be on."

I shrugged. I was a different person here than I was out there, yes, and very few people saw the real me. They wanted the larger-than-life, fun athlete, so that's what I gave them. But I wasn't interested in talking about that with Aurora. "We need to put the game on," I said, making my way for the remote on the coffee table, thankful to escape her line of questioning.

"You can't watch TV." She yanked the remote away from me.

I sighed. "Fine. I won't watch it. I'll just sit here and listen to it." I closed my eyes. "I need to know how Potter does. That kid's bat isn't where it should be, and we're making a playoff run this year."

"If I see you watching it or getting worked up, we're shutting it off."

"As long as they win, I won't get the least bit worked up," I promised. Cracking my eyes open again, I took her in. She was still dressed in the Revs polo and black pants she'd worn to work. "We're not going anywhere. Go get comfy."

"This is pretty much all I brought." She shrugged.

I cocked an eyebrow at her. "You didn't bring anything to change into?" She was staying for five days, and she'd only packed work clothes?

"Only pajamas, but I'm not putting those on." She averted her gaze and shifted on her feet.

"Give me a break." Sighing, I stomped to my bedroom in search of sweats and a T-shirt.

When I held them out to her, she looked from them to me and back again, a frown marring her pretty face.

"It's not like I haven't seen you in sweatpants and T-shirts before." I cocked a brow. I wasn't going to pretend we were strangers.

She huffed, but finally accepted the clothes. "Thanks."

I shook my head as she made her way to the guest room to change. When she stepped back into the living room, I froze. At the sight of her, my heart skipped off beat in my chest and my blood surged south. In sweatpants, I was at risk of very easily embarrassing myself, but with one quick shift, I hid the issue. What was it about her wearing my T-shirt that made my chest puff out? That, along with the dick problem and the sudden caveman urge to throw her over my shoulder and drag her to my room, was ridiculous. If she'd walked out in lingerie? Sure, I'd get the way my body had taken over. But she was standing before me in an oversized shirt that hid her body, with her purple toenail polish peeking out beneath the hem of my white sweats. As I took in the glasses and off-center messed bun, it hit me. The casual Aurora that stood in front of me now was more than just reminiscent of the girl I'd been obsessed with.

I swallowed hard. I understood the line in the sand. If

I made a move, she could lose a job she'd wanted her entire life. And I couldn't do that to her. So my focus needed to be on anything but the girl of my dreams who was currently tucking herself into the far side of the couch.

So I focused on the announcers, the play calling, the game. I leaned back so my head rested on the cushion behind me and closed my eyes. Oddly, I was hyped up and relaxed all at the same time. Honestly, if Aurora shifted over two cushions and curled into the crook of my arm, I might call tonight the best night I'd had in years.

It was ridiculous, since I had a concussion and couldn't play the game I loved, but it was true.

8

Rory

I TAPPED on the door lightly, but Mason made no sound. We'd talked about this, that I'd have to check on him a few times during the night, but still, I felt weird walking into his room. It was my job, so I took a deep breath, put on my big girl panties, and slowly pushed the door open.

The light from the hallway filtered around his room, highlighting the heavy wood furniture in the space. The top of his dresser was littered with two watches, his wallet and keys, his Revs badge, a slew of receipts, and a half-empty bottle of water. His T-shirt was draped on a chair by the window, and his sneakers and socks were on the floor. The clutter reminded me of the teenage Mason. His mom always picked at him for leaving a trail everywhere he went. Although the rest of the apartment was tidy, it was clear from the state of this room that he hadn't changed that much over the years.

On the king-size platform bed in the center of the room, he lay on his stomach, arms and legs spread, taking up the entire space. The bed was huge, but so was Mason. At six-four and almost two hundred and fifty pounds of muscle, the man was enormous. I continued my assessment of him as I tiptoed toward him. Halfway across the room, I realized how silly it was to move so quietly. After all, I was here to wake him. I shook my head at myself as I laid a hand on his bare shoulder.

A deep, throaty groan rumbled through him. Then he was pushing up onto the elbow of his good arm. The muscles of his upper arms rippled and bulged as he propped himself up.

I swallowed back the wave of attraction that hit me at the sight. He'd always been strong, but now, with his ripped biceps and shoulders on display like this, I was flooded with all kinds of thoughts I had no business thinking.

"Head's fine," he muttered. He was looking at me, scanning my face, though his eyes were out of focus. He continued his perusal, moving lower. When he got to my tank top, he blinked, and his gaze sharpened.

Shit, he was zeroing in on the thin material covering my braless breasts.

I fought a shiver, even as my nipples hardened under his scrutiny.

He wet his lips.

I might have stopped breathing.

Slamming his eyes shut, he locked his jaw. "Either climb in or get out. I swear to God, Aurora, I only have so much control."

I couldn't look away from his full lips as memories of them moving against mine floated through my mind. I could almost feel his hand cupping my neck and pulling me closer like it did all those years ago. Eleven years ago, he had been a good kisser. I could only imagine time had improved his skill.

I glided an inch closer, consumed by the need to feel his arms around me, before logic took over and I remembered why I was in here. My goal tonight was to wake him. Because I was currently being paid to watch him for concussion symptoms.

Backing away, I held my hands up, my chest heaving and short, staccato breaths escaping my lungs. I tripped over a shoe in the middle of the room, but righted myself before I could embarrass myself too badly. "Sorry," I muttered, and with that, I turned and fled the room.

For a long time, I lay in bed, unable to fall asleep. There were a dozen reasons why I shouldn't get involved with Mason. The most important of them all? My career. I couldn't just send out a few applications and get picked up by another team. Jobs like mine were highly sought after and difficult to get.

I was creating problems that didn't exist anyway. Mason and I were old friends. Nothing more. It wasn't worth stressing about my job one way or another. I just needed to ignore the mess of emotions that he was creating inside me.

I spun to my side and slid my hand under my pillow. With my eyes squeezed shut, I prayed for sleep. What felt like minutes after I finally dozed off, my alarm was going off, alerting me that it was time to check on him again.

This time, I wrapped a blanket around my shoulders before I shuffled to his bedroom door. I tapped his foot lightly, and when he moved, I hightailed it out of the room. But even if I'd avoided another encounter, sleep still eluded me.

The click of a cabinet closing pulled me from my fitful dreams, and when my brain came online enough to register where I was, the first thing I noticed was the scent of coffee. Coffee that Mason probably shouldn't be drinking.

I hauled my exhausted body out of bed, changed into my black pants and polo, and fixed my hair. Then I took a moment to breathe deeply and bolster my willpower. I was here to do my job. Nothing more. And that's what I'd do for the next few days. No more joking, no more books or reminiscing about old times. Just my job.

I opened the door and headed into the kitchen. Just as my feet hit the tile, I pulled up short.

The man was propped up against the counter, wearing nothing but grey sweats. He held his mug aloft and tipped it my way. "It's decaf," he said, as if he was prepared for my admonishment.

I refused to let my focus stray from his face. "Good."

"You hungry? Wanna grab breakfast?" He brought his mug to his lips and watched me over the top as he sipped.

"Like go out?"

"I don't have anything here." He shrugged and set his mug down.

As he did, I lost the battle I'd been fighting with myself and slowly took him in. His shoulders and his broad chest and his toned six-pack.

Damn, the man was perfect.

He smirked like he knew what I was thinking but was nice enough to not say anything.

"Damiano and Avery always talk about the banana pancake special on Tuesdays at the diner a few blocks away."

For a moment, I scanned the room. Going out to breakfast didn't feel like a work duty, but Dr. Anderson and Beckett had both made it clear that my only priority this week was to stick with Mason so I could keep an eye on him and rehab his shoulder. I supposed eating breakfast together fell into the keeping an eye on him category. "Okay."

"Let me get dressed." He stalked past me toward his room.

When he disappeared, I finally let myself relax. Yes, breakfast was a great idea. I needed to get out of his apartment. With every minute that passed here, it felt as though the walls were closing us in and forcing us closer, and I needed a bit of fresh air and space.

"Don't forget your sling," I called down the hall.

He popped his head out of his room and glowered at me. "I thought we established that I wasn't wearing that."

"I said you could take it off when you laid down to watch the game, not that you never had to put it back on." I stepped out into the hall and crossed my arms. "You want it to get better, don't you? Or would you rather worry about the pain that will shoot through you the next time someone crashes into you on the field?"

With a huff and a roll of his eyes, he shut his bedroom door behind him.

I let out a long breath. At least the weirdness was gone.

Twenty minutes later, he was shifting his arm in the sling and once again complaining.

"I am not a fan of this thing," he said as we walked toward the diner.

"Mason Dumpty." For at least the third time since we'd left his apartment, his name was being shouted. This time from across the street.

In a heartbeat, Mason's glower was replaced by a grin, and the fun-loving baseball guy Boston loved had returned. The fan jogged across the road, and after he snapped a selfie and gave Mason a fist bump, he was gone. It was impressive the way Mason could turn on his celebrity athlete persona like that. If I was constantly being interrupted, I'd get annoyed. In fact, I was trying not to be annoyed when the fifth person of the morning stopped us. Mason didn't seem bothered by it, even though all the attention stretched what should have been a ten-minute walk into thirty, and his stomach was growling so loud there was no way the last two fans hadn't heard it.

"We finally made it." Mason held the door open for me and waved me in.

Despite my best effort to remain unaffected by him, his boyish smirk had my stomach flipping over itself.

An older woman in a pink shirt with blue-gray hair smiled brightly as she moved toward us.

"Mason Dumpty." She clapped her hands. "Damiano and Knight stop in regularly. We wondered if you'd grace us with your presence one of these days."

"You must be Pam." Mason pointed to a photo on the wall of a short stack covered in whipped cream, fruit, and chocolate chips. "I keep hearing about you and these banana pancakes, so I thought I'd come by and see what all the fuss is about."

"Oh, you're in for a treat. Everyone loves our banana pancakes." She took him in, cocking one brow when her gaze landed on the sling. "That was one hell of a catch."

A smile lifted the corners of his mouth. "If only I could remember any of it."

"Aw, poor dear." She patted his good arm, then turned to me, like she'd just noticed me standing beside Mason. "And who's this?"

"My babysitter for the next week." He winked at me, then turned back to Pam. "She's pretty, isn't she?" he mock-whispered.

I shook my head and smiled at the older woman, but quickly dipped my chin, hoping to hide the way my cheeks heated in response to his teasing.

We followed Pam to our table, and when it was time to order, we both went with the banana pancake special. Throughout our meal, we were subjected to one curious glance after another. I tried to ignore them, but the scrutiny made me uneasy, especially as I shoved pancakes into my mouth, doing my best not to make a mess. Mason, on the other hand, seemed completely oblivious to it, or maybe he was just used to it.

Along with the looks, I did my best to ignore how much this felt like a date, especially when he paid. Maybe I should have put up a fight over the bill, but in the end, it was easier to let him.

So much for my vow to keep our relationship professional. As we left the diner, I told myself that from that moment on, I would do better.

9

Mason

WITH A GRUNT, I flipped the newspaper shut. The last two days had sucked.

No, that wasn't fair. I'd actually had fun hanging out with Aurora, but now I was worked up. Sometime after leaving the diner on Tuesday, she'd put up some serious walls around what was okay and what wasn't. She had to get close, had to touch me, when it was time for the stretches and exercises that my shoulder required. But during every other waking moment, she kept a six-foot bubble of space. And there were no more Harry Potter voices reading. Instead, she gave me a book or a newspaper so I could read on my own.

As much as I complained about the restrictions she and the team doc had put on me, my eyes were tired after just five minutes of reading. They got tired after ten minutes of playing cards. But at least I had stopped losing to her at rummy yesterday.

And the Revs were playing better too. Potter was no longer missing stupid catches, and he was batting well enough that the team was winning. Aurora had been letting me watch the games as long as I didn't jump up and down and scream at the TV. I'd done well not letting myself get worked up.

Until now.

Although it wasn't the Revs making me crazy.

After that intense moment in my bedroom a few nights ago, Aurora had been guarded. She'd kept our relationship strictly professional, which was something I'd typically appreciate. But with her, I didn't.

I was tempted to stand up and shout when she announced she was getting in the shower, because my mind could only think of one thing. Her naked body, slick with soap. Before now, she'd kept details like that to herself, so I'd had no idea when she had showered. I'd assumed she waited until one of many naps. I felt like toddler in that way. I could only make it a few hours without resting, because man, this concussion was exhausting. So drifting off on the sofa was my new norm.

Another new norm for me? Uncomfortable boners. It was like I was back in high school, pining over Aurora. Those days when, if she smiled at me, walked near me, or sat next to me, my dick sprang to life. I thought I'd grown out of the nonsense, but as it turned out, that pesky bad habit had only disappeared because Aurora was no longer around. And now that she was back in my life? I pretty much existed in varying degrees of hard.

She was supposed to be my friend, but friends didn't think about other friends spread out beneath them.

Friends didn't imagine what it'd be like to taste every inch of one another.

God, I was glad my teammates weren't around. They'd give me so much shit. Just like my high school friends had given me a hard time about how obsessed I was with the girl.

They'd never understood it. Back then, she was shy and quiet, not part of our world. She was into books, movies about dragons, and staying home on Friday nights. I'd always admired how little she worried about being cool. Even if we didn't hang out in the same circles, she wasn't off-limits. None of my friends were bothered by my crush on her.

But now? The Revs had strict rules about fraternization. Worse than that? If we broke those rules, I wasn't the one who would pay the price. No, I'd get a slap on the wrist, while she'd get fired.

I shook my head. I needed to get out of this apartment. Being in such close proximity to her was messing with my head. I was halfway down the hallway on my way to change when the guest bathroom door swung open and Aurora stepped out.

I froze, and every inch of me went on high alert. *Fuck.* I pinched my eyes closed, willing them to stay that way. And I was successful too, until the scent of her floral shampoo or body wash or God knew what she'd used on her naked, toned body wafted up and hit my nose. I zeroed in on her flushed cheeks first, then let my gaze drift lower. At the sight of her exposed skin glistening with a light sheen of moisture, all the blood in my body rushed south.

The towel she held in place shifted slightly as she cleared her throat, but she stood in the doorway, watching me like a deer caught in the headlights.

I thought I needed to get out of the apartment before, but that was nothing compared to the desire to flee that hit me as I stood just a few feet from a wet, mostly naked Aurora. "Let's go get lunch before my appointment with the doc," I rushed out.

She tilted her head to the side. "We just ate breakfast."

"C'mon. I'm suddenly ravenous." I took one more glance down at the swell of her breasts, then forced myself to brush past her. "Going to change."

If I stood there any longer, I'd do something stupid, like pin her to the wall and kiss the hell out of her.

So I stalked into my room and shut the door behind me, all the while trying to block out the temptation that had taken up residence in my guest room. The doctor had better clear me to be alone, because I couldn't do this for another day.

10

Rory

Mason was weird all the way through lunch, like the annoyance of the tension between us was getting to him blackening his mood, which was the opposite of his typical light heartedness. The only time he'd smiled was when fans had come over to ask for an autograph or snap a selfie. And now he was arguing with the doctor, which I knew he wanted space from our situation, but his acting irrational was causing the exact opposite reaction in the doctor.

"I'm absolutely fine to stay by myself, and I'm not wearing this thing anymore." With a huff, he yanked the sling off and tossed it onto the ground.

One of the primary symptoms of a concussion was moodiness, so if he wanted the doctor to think he was doing better he'd need to stop. Maybe if he wasn't being so difficult, the doctor wouldn't be insisting on another day of supervision.

"Our typical recommendation is four to five days, but I'd like to err on the side of caution and give it a couple more."

It was probably a wise move. The Revs were playing the Metros tonight, which meant it would be a close game. Mason would likely be more worked up than he had been for the last couple, and even when he was doing his best to rein it in, it was difficult for him not to react to the outcome of the game in a big way. Especially because it was clear that the team was struggling without him.

"Is she bad company?"

I might have bristled at the implication if not for the sympathy Dr. Anderson was silently telegraphing my way. Clearly, he thought I'd been dealing with this bad attitude for days.

"Do you want someone else?"

"No, no, not at all." Mason sighed. "I just want to be back on the field."

Dr. Anderson turned his attention back to me. "How's his shoulder?"

"It's fine." I stepped up and pulled up the notes I'd been keeping in my phone. "Range of motion is great, honestly. The sling is more for support and a reminder to his fans to take it easy when they approach him than it is to stabilize the shoulder. And he doesn't seem to have much pain." I glanced back at Mason. "His strength has mostly returned. Putting aside his head issues, I'd say he could be back on the field in three days."

Dr. Anderson rubbed his chin thoughtfully and assessed Mason.

"See? I can play in three days," Mason added.

The doctor's mouth turned down. "That would be the case if it was only your shoulder we were concerned about. Your head is still the bigger issue."

Mason threw his hands in the air. "I can't just sit around and do nothing."

Dr. Anderson arched a brow, obviously used to pushback like this. "Let's start with some light cardio—"

"Like running the bases?" Mason sat up straighter, and his face brightened.

I stopped myself from rolling my eyes. I'd stay out of this argument.

An exasperated huff left the doctor's mouth. "No. No impact. Walking only. To get your heart rate up. Like a stroll around the harbor."

Unsurprisingly, Mason's mouth instantly turned down into a frown.

"You gotta start somewhere, Mason," I reminded him. "We'll go together."

Bowing his head, he laced his fingers in front of him. "I just miss having the outlet. Not playing makes me antsy."

My heart ached at his admission. I had to remind myself that his surly attitude was justified. He lived his life for the game, and now we were telling him he had to wait longer to get back to it.

"It's common for athletes to miss the adrenaline rush." Dr. Anderson looked up from his notes. "What do you do in the offseason to deal with it?"

Mason put his hands on the bench on either side of

him and shifted, keeping his chin tucked. "Pickup basketball, trivia night...sex."

The doctor chuckled. "No basketball yet, but either of the other two would be fine." Then he turned to look at me. "It would be okay for you to head home for the night if he's got a date. Just come back in the morning."

This was all relatively routine. Athletes usually asked about sex pretty quickly after an injury. Typically, I didn't think much of it. But in this moment? Though it wasn't fair or reasonable, my heart raged at the idea of Mason going on a date. He and I were nothing more than athlete and trainer, so I had no right to be upset.

"Sure." I nodded at the doctor. "No problem. I'll make sure I'm out of the way."

In my periphery, Mason gritted his teeth, but I kept my attention averted, hoping he couldn't see the way this conversation had affected me.

"Great." Dr. Anderson snapped the chart shut. "Then I'll see you in two days." He shook Mason's hand. "Call me if you need anything, Rory."

I nodded again, and then he was gone.

Mason crossed his arms over his navy T-shirt, finally garnering my attention. "Do you really think I'd send you home so I could hook up with some random girl?"

I took a deep breath, ignoring the lancing pain in my chest. "Athletes tend to have higher-than-average sex drives. To help deal with the frustration of injury, it's common to use sex as a release."

He pushed off the examination bench and stood only inches from me, forcing me to look up at him. The scent of his pine cologne hit my nose just as the heat of his body wrapped around me and made my core clench. He wasn't touching me, but he might as well have been.

"That's all true. But you're forgetting one important detail, *Aurora*."

I fought the shiver that threatened to run down my spine at the sound of my name on his lips, but there was no stopping the goose bumps that broke out on my arms.

He noticed the reaction. Of course he did. And he ran a finger along my pebbled skin from my wrist to my elbow, making my heart rate pick up speed.

"There is only one woman stuck in my head." His jade green eyes burned into my own, and the air between us thrummed. "So there is no way I could touch anyone else."

I sucked in a quick breath. No matter how much physical and figurative space I'd tried to put between us over the last few days, this heavy level attraction had continued to hover like a fog. I was locked in his sights, helpless to escape this ensnarement.

But with a blink, he stepped back and cleared his throat, and the tether between us slackened.

"So let's go for a fucking walk." Mason yanked his Boston Bolts hat off the exam table and pulled it low over his eyes. Then he headed toward the exam room door and held it open for me.

It was a gorgeous June day. The air wasn't too hot or muggy, but it was warm enough to spend the day outside in short sleeves.

We'd been walking in silence for a solid ten minutes before I worked up the nerve to speak. "You sure you're okay?"

"Yeah." He roughed a hand over his jaw and tugged his hat down low again. "I'm just frustrated. Usually, I take all this out on the field, so not being out there only makes it that much harder." He shook his head. "And as much as I say my head is good. I'm not in a place where I could win at bar trivia yet either, so that would just annoy me."

That I understood, he didn't even lose at cards well. I had thrown the last few games in an effort to keep him chill.

"Want to check out the zoo?" He nodded at the sign for the Boston Zoo ahead.

I couldn't help the confused frown that tugged on my lips. "You want to go to the zoo?"

"Yeah, why not?" He shrugged and side-eyed me. "Come on, it'll be fun. We could see Puff."

"I don't understand what all the excitement over that bird is about."

"He's our team bird." Under the bill of his hat, his face lit in a smile. "Come on. Once you see him, you'll understand. You're gonna love him."

I very much doubted that.

11

Mason

WALKING around the Boston Zoo with Aurora quickly lifted my spirits. I loved spending time with her, and this change of scenery was what I needed to adjust my attitude. I had to stop being so difficult, otherwise I worried that Dr. Anderson would question her abilities. She was great at what she did. I was the problem here. And despite how cranky I'd been, I wouldn't want anyone else here with me. So I was determined to chill and enjoy our time together.

She had drawn her lines, and until she gave me signals that she wanted more, I'd respect that this was a platonic day of fun. I'd done that more times than I could count in high school. I should be used to it.

Rather than wander and look at the other animals, I led Aurora straight to the Puffin Penguin house.

"Even the sign has a baseball on it," she mused, her chin tipped up as she regarded the sign that hung above the door. The image Gianna, Dragon's sister, had designed was of a puffin with a baseball and a penguin with a hockey puck.

I chuckled. "Puff's a Rev, remember?" I pulled the door open and stood back so she could enter the huge space in front of me. The viewing area was large, but the majority of the space in the building was for the animals. Behind the floor-to-ceiling glass was an expanse of water and rocks. It only took a minute to find Puff. He was easy to pick out because of the blue and white friendship bracelet around his leg.

"Is he wearing a beaded bracelet?" Aurora asked beside me.

I chuckled and stepped closer to the glass. "Yup. Dragon wears one that matches. They never take them off."

She tilted her chin and watched me through narrowed eyes like she couldn't decide whether I was messing with her.

With a tap on the glass, I got Puff's attention, and the little guy waddled our way. I hadn't expected to feel so relieved when I set foot in this place, but already, being here with Puff made me feel like I was with the team. When he approached, he tapped on the glass with his beak, imitating me. I stole a glance at Aurora to make sure she was watching. The sweet smile she gave me made my stomach tighten. Damn. The need to impress her, to make her laugh, was all consuming.

Everything about her was consuming me. But her job mattered, and I respected that I couldn't cross her lines. Those lines, though, didn't include making her laugh.

Turning back to the puffin on the other side of the glass, I waved a hand. In response, he bobbed his head from side to side.

Aurora brought her fingers to her lips and giggled. "Are you doing that?"

Holding back a smirk, I shrugged, but then I made a circle in the air with one finger.

Her eyes widened as Puff dove into the water and swam in a complete circle. "Are you making that bird dance?"

"Yeah." I couldn't help but smile at the little guy. "They're really trainable."

She watched him with a softness in her expression I'd never seen, then scanned the rest of the birds before she caught sight of the plaque off to the side of the glass that credited the Revs for Puff's exhibit. "Did you all really donate this?"

"Yeah." I lifted a brow. "Dragon pretty much made us. He's obsessed with Puff Daddy."

Avery, Dragon's girlfriend, appeared behind Aurora then, her hands on her hips. "Are you torturing my bird?"

"No, of course not."

Her response was a huff and a roll of her eyes.

I bit back a smirk. "Big day's coming up soon, right?"

Dragon had been talking nonstop about Puff and his girl and the eggs that were set to hatch soon.

"Yep. We've got less than two weeks now." Avery nodded. "We moved the nest into the back. The dads were getting a little agitated with so many people coming in. Made everyone happier."

"How many babies are there?" Aurora asked, eyeing

the birds a little warily. Although she'd smiled and laughed at Puff's antics, her shoulders were pulled up a little, and she kept scanning the rocks and the water like she might be a bit uncomfortable.

"Puff and Puffette have three, and another couple has two. If all goes well, we'll have five new residents soon." Avery turned to me and gave me a sympathetic smile. "How are you feeling? Chris said you were really out of it the other day after the game."

"Yeah." I ducked my head. "I actually don't remember much."

"Oh." She took a small step back and quickly changed the conversation, as if she'd picked up on my unease and understood that I didn't want to talk about it. "Did you guys want to see him? I can get him out."

"Out?" Aurora's eyes widened almost comically, like the idea was insane. "Yeah, no, I'm good."

"You have a thing about birds or something?" I didn't remember that from high school, but we spent most of our time together studying inside, so maybe it never came up.

"I wouldn't call it 'a thing.'" A cute little line appeared between her brows as she waved at the glass. "I just like them better in there." Then she fought a shudder.

"You're afraid of birds." I laughed, shaking my head.

"I'm not afraid of birds." The way she shifted on her feet and wrung her hands belied that statement. "They're cute. Through the glass or, like, at a distance." She swallowed thickly and frowned. "I don't need to hang out with them near me."

I laughed at the way she practically cringed at those

last words. When I caught Avery watching the back-and-forth between us, wearing a very speculative expression, though, I schooled my features.

Shit.

The last thing I needed was for her to assume there was something going on between Aurora and me. If she told her dad, there would be hell to pay. Coach was a stickler for rules.

"Did you guys want to grab lunch?" Avery asked as she continued to scrutinize us.

"I think we're going to walk around the zoo a bit." I shot Aurora a smirk. "It's my *allowed* exercise for the day."

She rolled her eyes at me but gave Avery a sweet smile and agreed that we'd better continue on.

As we were walking away from Puff's exhibit, I bumped her with my arm. "What do you want to see now? Stay away from the birds, huh?"

"Shut up." She huffed out a chuckle. "And be careful with your shoulder."

"It really feels fine, babe."

She stiffened next to me. Babe probably crossed some of those lines she set up. I was about to apologize when she went on.

"Yeah, because of me. Clearly, I'm the only one of us who's concerned about keeping it that way." She shot me a glower that was hard to take seriously with the way her blond hair bounced as she walked. Now I wasn't sure if she was mad about babe or my shoulder, but I couldn't help but smile.

I should probably feel bad, but her exasperation with me was so damn cute I couldn't help it.

I wrapped my arm around her waist and pulled her in close. "Thanks for looking out for me."

With a whack to my stomach, she freed herself from my hold and continued on. We had just stepped up to a sea lion enclosure when one popped up, water sluicing down its head.

Rory sighed, grasping the railing in front of us. "They're so cute."

The animal nodded like he was agreeing with her and flapped one flipper, sending a spray of water into the air.

I chuckled at its antics, but Aurora jumped away from the shower and scooted closer. And damn if I could stop the instinct to wrap my arms around her. Not that my hold could shelter her from the splash, but having her in my arms felt right.

Her soft floral scent hit me as her soft hair brushed my cheek, tempting me to hold her just a second longer and take a breath of her into my lungs. Having her this close made my stomach tighten and my chest feel heavy. Even as she pushed away, I didn't want to let her go.

But she smiled and grabbed my arm, as if she hadn't felt the pull between us too, and dragged me away, leaving the guy to splash a couple who'd just appeared. "I don't want to get soaked. Come on."

All day, her reactions made me laugh. She squealed when the tiger came out and paced along the glass. She giggled at the swinging monkey. Joy lit her face when she hand-fed the giraffes. But she surprised the hell out of me when she suggested we stop to see the snakes and reptiles.

This woman was afraid of birds, but not snakes?

I'd been to the zoo more than a few times, considering my teammate's obsession with both Puff and Avery. However, I'd never had so much fun. Even if this wasn't a date. She might be here with me because she was required to be, but it sure felt like a date. Especially when I bought her a stuffed animal on our way out.

"It's the perfect bird. The kind you don't have to be afraid of." I chuckled as I handed her the fluffy black and white puffin wearing a throwback Revs jersey.

"Thanks." With a sigh, she snuggled the bird against her chest. "I'm never gonna live this down, am I?"

"Nope." I led her toward the exit. "Were you always afraid of birds? I don't remember—"

"I am not afraid of birds." She cut me off.

"Hey, Dumpty," a fan called, heading my way.

I'd escape being noticed for the most part today, but apparently, my luck had run out. So with my happy outfielder smile firmly in place, I high-fived both fans and signed their zoo maps.

"Do you ever get tired of it?" Aurora asked after they were out of earshot.

My typical answer was *hell no; I love what I do*, but I didn't want to lie to her.

"All the damn time, but when they see me, they expect the larger-than-life outfielder, and that's what they deserve. They buy my jersey and show up to see me play, and in return, I show up for them." Fighting back the need to wince at the throb that had started over the last few minutes, I rubbed at my temple. Then I straightened my hat and pulled it lower, hoping it would keep others from recognizing me. "Even on my bad days, they get happy Mason."

"You have a headache?" She stepped in closer and rubbed circles on my back.

Her touch alone eased some of the tension.

"It's not horrible, but kinda," I admitted. Telling her the truth, showing her my vulnerabilities, was easy, when, for the rest of the world, I hid behind a smile.

"Let's get an Uber." She pulled out her phone and unlocked the screen. "We can go home and get something to eat."

At the idea of going home with this woman, my first thought was *hell yeah*. But this wasn't a date, even if it felt like one. With each passing day, though, it was harder to remember that.

12

Rory

"Thank you."

As Mason stepped out of the Uber behind me, I assessed him, confused. What was he thanking me for? He'd insisted on paying for the rideshare as well as admittance to the zoo.

"I was frustrated about not being able to work out and about still being on IR." He shrugged. "But I had a good time today. Just being with you took my mind off what I can't do."

"Yeah, it was fun." It had felt like a date. Hell, it had been better than any date I'd ever been on. Yet it wasn't one. For days, I'd been fighting the pull between us. I'd been tense and guarded, which had made it hard to enjoy hanging out with him. But at some point today, all those worries had slipped away.

As we headed to the entrance of his building, he rested a hand on the small of my back. Though I knew I should, I didn't push it away. The warmth of his palm soaked into me, making heat curl in my core. His pine scent only amplified the dangerous feelings I was having toward him.

I was lost in thoughts of Mason when a flash of gray caught my eye and forced me to focus on my surroundings. When I did, my heart leaped into my throat, and I jumped back. Because there was a bird headed straight for us. I collided with a wall of muscle, tucking my head into his chest, and squeezed him and the stuffed puffin with all my strength.

"It's just a pigeon," Mason mumbled into my hair, looping an arm around me fully. "But don't worry, I've got you."

His deep voice rumbled through me, causing me to shiver. Slowly, I looked up, only to find him already watching me. His gaze burned into me, and my skin heated under his scrutiny. Without breaking eye contact, he tilted forward, bringing his face closer to mine. And I couldn't pull away. Didn't want to. But...

"You know we can't do this," I whispered when his mouth was so close I could practically taste him.

"Maybe we shouldn't," he said, his breath rushing over my lips, "but I need to kiss you more than I need my next breath."

The heat in his eyes burned bright, and the world around us disappeared. He cupped my face in both hands and continued what he'd started, moving in closer and pressing his mouth to mine.

On contact, I brought a hand to his pec, and a deep sigh escaped me. As if something I'd been missing had finally returned to me. He licked at the seam of my lips, and when I opened for him, his tongue darted in, stroking my own, and I melted into his embrace.

Mason growled as he pulled back, almost like he hated that he had to. "Inside," he whispered, his chest rumbling under my palm.

"Yeah." I nodded, still dazed. Though I was alert enough to realize that we shouldn't be doing this on the sidewalk in broad daylight.

He turned me, the move dislodging my puffin, but he caught it in midair. Then, with one hand on the stuffed bird and one hand low on my back, he led me into the building. He only gave the valet a quick nod as he rushed me onto the elevator. The second the silver doors slid shut behind us, he yanked me into the hard plane of his chest and slammed his lips to mine in a bruising kiss. The groan that reverberated through him as he took the kiss deeper sent a shiver racing down my spine.

Digging his fingers into my hips tightly, he backed me up against the wall. And as the feeling of the cool stainless steel at my back warred with the heat of him at my front, I wrapped my arms around his neck and pulled him closer. He skated his hands down my sides, then cupped my ass and lifted me so I could wrap my legs around him. His tongue tangled with mine as he explored every inch of my mouth. Whimpering, I tightened my hold on his neck, needing him closer. But instead of obeying, he pulled back suddenly.

I blinked, and my stomach sank. Was he putting a stop to this? After I'd finally given in? But then I realized the door behind him was open. Oh. With a deep breath in, I dropped my legs from around his waist. Begrudgingly, he released me. Though once we'd stepped into the hall, that hand was on the small of my back again.

He groaned from behind me as we moved down the hall, the sound making heat pool low in my belly.

"We need a bed," he mumbled, adding to the desire already taking over.

When I glanced over my shoulder, his focus was locked on my ass.

But as he opened the door to his apartment, questions swirled in his green irises.

He was giving me a chance to tell him he was being presumptuous. But I wanted this as much as he did.

"I've waited eleven years for this." He ran his tongue across his lower lip, studying my face. "But if you're not sure…"

I stepped forward, pressing a palm to his chest. "I'm sure." Popping up on my toes, I brushed my lips against the rough skin of his neck.

The shudder that worked its way through him filled me with a sense of power. Knowing I could make this man shiver gave my confidence a huge boost.

Keeping my lips against his skin, I said, "I want you."

His pulse pounded below my lips.

"Badly," I whispered.

His groan vibrated through me, and in a heartbeat, I was backed against the closed door, with his arms braced on either side of my head.

His lips were a breath away from mine, but he didn't close the distance. "Oh, I intend to give you everything you want, baby. But be prepared, because I'm going to take my time with you." He examined every inch of my face, then perused my body as well. Each flick of his eyes felt like a promise of what was to come. "I want to taste every part of you. Fuck, I've wanted this body for years."

"Good." A smile curved my lips in response to the need in his voice.

I ran my hands through his hair as his skimmed down my sides and bit into my ass with a pain that was so full of pleasure, it pulled a moan from deep within me. He lifted me like that and carried me toward his bedroom. His mouth was on mine again in another desperate kiss that I couldn't get enough of. But then I was falling. My stomach flipped just as I landed on his soft mattress.

Running my tongue over my bottom lip, I propped myself up on my elbows and watched as he toed off his shoes and pulled his T-shirt over his head.

God, he was gorgeous. I soaked in the view of his broad shoulders and the expanse of lean, tanned muscle. I swallowed hard, itching to touch him.

In quick movements, he tugged his shorts and boxers off, and when his cock sprang free, the heat simmering low in my core ignited. Chest heaving suddenly, I sat up and tugged at the hem of my shirt. Because, while Mason was utterly naked, I was still fully clothed.

He moved in close and gently pushed my hands away. "No. Let me."

Obediently, I dropped my hands to the bed. Mason leaned over me, his fingers brushing the sensitive skin of my stomach as he lifted my shirt over my head. My heart rate picked up as his heated stare burned into me again. When my shirt had hit the floor, he slid his hands down my back and unhooked my bra, sending shivers of anticipation down my spine.

He pulled back, taking my bra with him, and when my breasts fell free, the way he looked at me had my cheeks heating.

"You are so damn beautiful." He tilted forward again, kissing the corner of my mouth. "So perfect." He worked his way down the column of my throat, then down my chest, his tongue tracing the curve of my breast.

He was teasing me, exploring me with his mouth. He moved lower, letting his tongue explore my belly before pulling my shorts and thong down my legs. When I was bare before him, his eyes blazed with that deep green I was quickly becoming addicted to all over again.

"Need you, Mason." We'd lost our chance at this eleven years ago, and now the need between us was stifling.

He slipped his hands under my knees and gave a quick tug, sending me falling back onto the mattress. Then he dragged his nose along my inner thigh, the move making me buck and moan. He stopped and pressed a kiss close to where I needed him most.

"I need to taste you." His tone was low, dark, desperate.

I shivered in response, wanting everything he was offering. But right now, what I needed most was to feel him. "I need you inside me."

He swiped his tongue along my center, teasing.

I whimpered and writhed. "Please."

"Since you asked so nicely." With a grin, he pushed to his feet. Then he opened his nightstand drawer and pulled out a condom. "But next time, I'm getting my mouth on you first."

He rolled the condom on and climbed on the bed between my legs. With one hand planted on the mattress beside my shoulder, he hovered over me, toying with me, swiping his tip up and down and coating himself in my wetness.

I hooked my legs around his waist and dug my heels into those divots of muscle right above his ass, forcing him closer. "Okay."

Jaw tense, he locked eyes with me and dipped his head a little closer. "You're sure?"

I nodded. "I'm sure." I'd never been more sure of anything in my whole life.

He entered me in one long thrust, filling me perfectly and forcing a scream from my throat.

As if he was thinking the same thing, he let out a muttered curse and gritted out, "Perfect. So perfect."

I cupped his stubbled cheek and tilted my hips, urging him on. In response, he leaned forward and molded his lips to mine. Then, as he deepened the kiss, he started to move. With each thrust, pressure built low in my belly.

Digging my fingers into the flesh of his shoulders, I matched his movements, lifting my hips to meet his. My core tightened, and the low burning heat inside me ramped up to full-fledged flames.

He picked up his pace, thrusting faster, harder, his cock hitting that spot inside me over and over. A flick of Mason's thumb across my clit, and pleasure ripped through my body, sensation after sensation shooting through me.

I was still lost in the high of my orgasm when Mason came with my name on his lips. As we came back down together, he collapsed on top of me. For a moment, he stayed like that, but as I sucked in one deep breath, then another, he rolled to his side, taking me with him. My chest heaved as I focused on regulating my breathing.

Mason pressed his lips to my temple. Then he pushed to his feet and smiled down at me. "Be right back."

I nodded, mimicking his smile, but my heart was already aching and my stomach was already sinking. Because what we'd just done couldn't happen again. God, did I want it to, but I couldn't work for the team and be with him. Even if we both wanted it. There were rules against that.

When he came back into the bedroom, he pulled me up and looped his arms around me, holding me close. "What's wrong?" he asked, pressing a kiss to my nose.

I swallowed hard and averted my gaze. "We can't do this again." I hated to say the words out loud. I very much wanted more time with Mason—more teasing, more laughing, more talking and touching—but we couldn't.

"Why not?" He pulled back, his brows pulled low and frustration simmering in his expression.

"We can't both work for the Revs and be together. It's not allowed." I sighed and lowered my head. "I can't lose my job, Mason."

"Hey." He slipped two fingers under my chin and tipped my face up so I was forced to look at him. "I would never let that happen." His look of intense earnestness made me want to believe his declaration. But the truth of the matter was that it wasn't really within his control.

He guided me back to the bed and wrapped an arm around me. As he rubbed small, soothing circles on my stomach, I stared at the ceiling.

If it came down to it, he brought in the fans. The Revs had sold more Dumpty jerseys than any other Rev this year. No one would get rid of that guy. They were franchise players. The guy management would bend over backward to keep because he was the kind of player who would retire with his number on a wall.

I looked over at Mason. That's exactly who he was.

And I was the brand-new trainer who could be replaced in a heartbeat.

He could dream all he wanted, but when push came to shove, my job was the one on the line.

Was I willing to give it up for him? I hated that I didn't know.

13

Mason

ROLLING OUT MY SHOULDER, I pushed the door to the locker room open with my good arm. Normally, stepping into this room felt like coming home. The navy carpet and built-in wooden lockers made the place feel warm and welcoming. The couches surrounding the huge circle logo were the perfect place to chill before games. Seeing my own space, with my name, was a comfort. Today's pinstripe uniform hung just below the shelf with my mitt. A few pairs of cleats sat on the floor at the bottom of the locker. Even the chair, the one I'd put a decal on so it was easily distinguishable—the original Revs Logo, of course, with the drum and stars.

Except—

"Looks who's finally back." Bosco slapped my good shoulder.

Ignoring him, I approached my locker, scanning the area around it in search of my chair.

"I bet you're happy to be here," he said from behind me.

"What did you do with it?"

He thought this dumbass game was funny. At first, he'd taken the chair, and I'd almost fallen trying to sit on it. Then he'd just scoot it closer to him, so he'd have two. That's when I put the decal on it, so it stood out as mine. Then it started showing up all over the locker room. Once I'd even found it in the shower.

Beside me now, he rocked back on his heels and smirked at me.

The fucker.

I scanned the room, but the chair was nowhere to be seen.

"I will find it, and then you will be sorry," I warned.

Bosco broke out in a fit of laughter.

Price, our catcher, joined in from across the room. "I bet you won't."

Despite my annoyance, I couldn't help but smile. It was good to be back. Thank fuck my head was on straight again and I'd been cleared to play.

The only dark spot in all of it was that Aurora had gone home after the doctor cleared me yesterday. The second she was gone, my apartment, which I usually loved, felt empty.

Even worse, my bed was cold. Her words—*we can't do this again*—put a damper on the night she'd spent with me. But I'd proved her wrong. I'd spent that night with my mouth on her, and my fingers and my cock inside her. I'd brought her to orgasm so many times I'd lost count. And even though she'd left saying it was over, her eyes said it wasn't.

"It's the best day ever. Humpty's back!" Knight cheered, pulling me out of my own head. "Want a good-luck hug?"

"A what?"

Knight stepped forward, tripping on something imaginary. He threw his arms out, but it did no good. Stumbling like a fawn who was learning to walk, he face-planted into my bad shoulder.

A shot of pain tore through me, but I fought the urge to wince or curse. The injury was still slightly bothering me and tight at times, but I was keeping that information to myself.

"A good-luck hug." Knight wrapped his arms around me and patted my back like I was a damn infant.

"Jesus," Damiano huffed. "Personal space, man."

Bosco snickered, and Knight smiled like a goofy jackass. This was the status quo around here. And it was why I loved these guys.

But how would I choose between them and Aurora if it came to that? Because she was right. We couldn't be together while we both worked for the Revs.

"You okay?" Eddie Martinez, our shortstop, cocked a worried brow my way.

"Yeah, yeah." I waved him off. "All good."

For now, all I could do was push thoughts of Aurora to the back of my mind and focus. Lock into the game and settle into being the Mason Dumpty my team and the fans expected.

That's what I did all through the pregame and warm-ups. My thoughts didn't stray to her again until a long fly popped up in the third inning, and flashes of the last time I was out here going after a ball hit me.

They were followed by fragments of memories. Of my week with her, the laughs, her smile, the way she felt in my arms, under me.

"Dumpty, you got it?"

Bosco's voice jarred me out of my thoughts and brought me back to the play. I sprinted toward him and stretched my arm out, ready to snag the ball out of the air. The move tweaked my shoulder, but I fought the wince once again. If Coach Wilson saw that I was hurting, I'd be back to riding the bench. So I breathed through the pain and forced a smile to my face as my glove snapped around the ball.

The crowd roared. Two outs.

I did my shuffle—pulling my arms in and lifting my shoulders, letting them bounce while I crisscrossed along the outfield with the ball in my glove. The sound system blasted, all bass, and I spun on the beat. God, I loved playing it up. And I could guarantee Knight was over at third doing his own. I turned that way and found him spinning. And our mascots—three Revolutionary War soldiers wearing Revs jerseys over their regimental coats—jumped up and joined us in the dance.

When the seats they'd been sitting in were empty, I caught sight of the sticker on one of the chairs. With a brow arched, I pointed to Bosco, then the chair.

His only response was a laugh so boisterous I could hear it over the music.

With a smirk, I tossed the ball to Martinez at short

and then subtly rolled out my shoulder. Luckily, the next batter went down swinging, giving me a break. When I stepped to the plate two innings later, I was loose and ready. The perfect pitch slid straight down the center, above home plate. Easy pickings. My bat collided with the leather, sending a crack vibrating up my arms. My shoulder burned, but I smiled as the ball flew high and straight over the outer wall.

Every step around the bases had my shoulder tightening, and by the time I made my way back to the dugout, I couldn't fight the grimace anymore.

The instant I hit that last concrete step, Coach, blue eyes narrowed like he's bracing for a fight, said, "You're done."

I didn't have it in me to argue. Not this time. So I lowered my head and gave him a small nod.

"Your shoulder's tight," he continued, like it hadn't registered that I'd agreed so easily. "Go see Rory."

As much as I hated to be pulled from the game, a thrill still raced through me at that last command. As much as I needed ice and some stim, I was most interested in the person who'd be working on me. In a matter of a week, she'd once again become my favorite person on the planet. The three-run homer I'd just added to our two-run lead gave us a nice cushion and had me feeling okay with sitting out for the rest of the game.

I made my way down the long tunnel that led to the locker room with only my girl in mind. We had left things unfinished when she went home, but one look at her, and my world was right again. That instant reaction told me all I needed to know. I stepped into the training room and clicked the door shut behind me.

The quiet sound had her looking up from the clipboard in her hands. She searched me, a crease forming between her brows, and her lips parted. "What—"

I pinned her to the wall and dropped my mouth to hers, effectively cutting her off and thoroughly devouring her. Had it only been a day? It felt like I'd gone weeks without tasting her. She was the perfect flavor, made just for me. I couldn't get enough of her lips on mine.

"I fucking miss you," I mumbled against her mouth.

She pulled back, her eyes wide and her breath coming in hard puffs between us. "We're not supposed to be doing this."

"I don't believe that, and neither do you."

She huffed and hit me with the cutest glower. She wanted to deny it, but I could see it in her eyes. She couldn't fight the pull between us either.

I molded my lips to hers again, content to stand here all day and kiss her.

Yeah. Baseball was fun, and I loved my teammates, but when it came to where I wanted to be? There was no contest. I didn't want to choose, but if I had to, I'd pick Aurora every damn time.

14

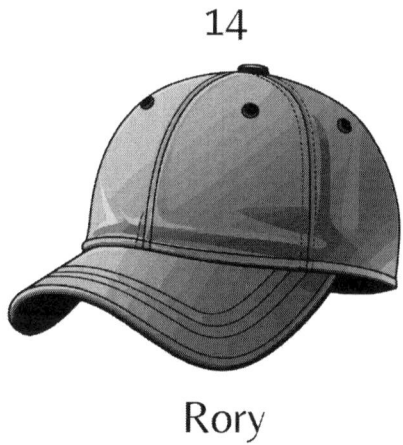

Rory

WE SHOULDN'T BE DOING *this*. Especially here. But no part of me wanted to push him away. In fact, even as I was telling myself we should stop, I was pulling him closer, pressing my breasts into the thick wall of his chest. What was it about him that was so irresistible?

"Come over tonight," he muttered against my lips. He tilted his head, taking my mouth deeper. The move caused his hat to fall to the floor.

I raked a hand through the hair at the back of his head. "I can't." *I shouldn't*. We needed lines. Boundaries. And one obvious one should involve no kissing him in the training room.

When he ran his tongue along my lower lip, I all but melted into him, forgetting all about that specific boundary.

But damn, he'd looked hot strutting in here, still dressed in his pinstripes. He was taller in his cleats, so I had to push up onto to my toes and stretch to wrap my arms around his neck.

The sharp knock had us jumping apart. I banged my hip into the exam table, and Mason took a big step back. He was running a hand over his face when the door opened and Cortney Miller, the team's GM, came into view.

He looked from Mason to me, then to the baseball cap on the ground between us. The blond giant ducked his head and stepped inside, wearing an unreadable expression.

Was it obvious to him what we had been doing?

A ripple of fear ran through me, taking with it all the desire and elation I'd felt when Mason was kissing me. Subtly, hoping he wouldn't notice, I pulled on my polo shirt, adjusting it.

"What's the verdict?" Cortney cocked his head in Mason's direction before turning toward me. "How bad is it?" His eyes were filled with a curiosity that had to do with more than just Mason's shoulder.

"Oh. Um..." He'd had me pinned against the wall a moment before Cortney appeared, so it couldn't be that bad. But I couldn't say that. "Seems fine. But I haven't gotten to do a full exam yet."

"Huh." He pressed his lips together like he was fighting a smile and cocked a brow as he surveyed us both again.

My knees wobbled under his scrutiny. Oh God. How long had Mason been in here? Probably long enough for me to have checked his freaking shoulder by now. He'd been pulled mid-game, so clearly, there was an issue. But

I hadn't even considered it when he walked through the door.

Cortney bent, grabbed Mason's hat off the ground, and tossed it to him. "You dropped this."

Mason caught it. "Thanks." His expression was one of complete calm. He was breathing easily, and his lips were tipped up just a little, like they always were when he was playing his part as Mason Dumpty, star center fielder. How was it possible for him to be so composed? My heart was beating so hard Cortney could probably hear it from the other side of the room. And Mr. Calm, Cool, and Collected over there just tipped his chin and muttered an easy "thanks." Ugh.

"Uh," I said, racking my brain for a reasonable response so I wouldn't look like a silent idiot. "We were going to try to put some heat on it before I looked at it. He didn't want me to touch it."

Cortney's eyebrow rose even higher, and he turned back to Mason. "Oh?"

His silent one-shoulder shrug was no help to me at all. Again, the man was totally chill while I was about to jump out of my skin. The need to confess and apologize was ridiculous. Cortney hadn't asked about anything besides how Mason's shoulder was. How was it even possible to give someone the third degree without saying a word? From what I'd heard, he had a teenage stepson who was all kinds of trouble, so I supposed he'd gotten good at interrogations. I needed to get out of the room before I spilled my guts.

"I'm just going to go grab the heat pack." With my head down, I scurried past Cortney and out of the training room. I couldn't even look at him. But when I came back in, I wished I hadn't left at all.

"Aurora was going to help me stretch it out. After the heat." He emphasized his statement by rolling his shoulder.

I kept my face neutral and my focus fixed on the heat pack, hoping I wasn't giving anything away. But no one called me by my formal name here. From day one, I'd introduced myself as Rory.

"It does make sense to bring a trainer with us on the away stretch. And you're saying you'd like *Rory* to accompany us, right?" A smirk lifted Cortney's lips, and I had to bite back a groan. "Or were you referring to someone else?"

"Nope. She's perfect."

My face flamed as I draped the hot pad over Mason's shoulder.

"Perfect, huh?"

"Yup." Mason lifted his chin unapologetically, and the ass didn't so much as flinch when I pinched his side as I settled the pack. He couldn't say things like that.

Rather than calling us out, Cortney, to my relief, moved on. "Okay, then. I'll run it by Beckett. Don't think he'll care."

"Yeah, where is the control freak? I'm surprised he's not here."

"Finn has T-ball."

"Already training the next generation of Langfields, huh?" Mason shook his head and chuckled. "It makes sense for him to even things out, I guess, since half of his siblings play hockey."

They did. Two of Beckett's brothers played for the Bolts, and the third owned the team. When I graduated and was looking for a job, working with the Bolts had been my first choice. I'd been thrilled when a position opened up with them, and I'd nearly passed out from excitement when I got a call from the Langfields. I'd hid my disappointment when I discovered the Revs were hiring rather than the Bolts, because a chance to work with either team was a huge deal. But I'd always been a hockey girl. I'd grown up in Cali, but I'd been a Bolts fan my whole life. And Dad would have died if I'd found a job with any hockey team. Which was why I'd applied for a few more positions elsewhere, even after getting this job with the Revs.

But suddenly, as I studied Mason, the thought of leaving Boston didn't sit well.

Cortney's phone buzzed in his hand, and after a quick glance at it, he focused on me again. "Email me the full report on the shoulder, okay, Rory?" Then he was gone.

Once it was just the two of us again, I blew out a relieved breath. But one look at Mason, and I kind of wanted to throttle him. The smile on his face made it obvious he thought the whole thing was comical.

"I hate you," I grumbled.

"Does that mean you're not coming over tonight?"

15

Mason

AURORA DIDN'T, in fact, come over after the game. She said she didn't have time since she had to pack for this stupid plane ride. How long could it take to shove shit into a bag? Especially since she wore the same thing every day—black pants and a polo with the Revs logo embroidered on it. Damn, did I love her ass in those pants, and the way her tits pulled on the buttons on the polo was perfection. And she looked great in blue. The image of her helped take away some of the frustration I felt over her absence last night.

But not all of it. And I'd done my best to convince her via whiney texts all evening. There was no reason she couldn't pack a bag, then spend the night at my place.

But the woman refused. And now she was ignoring my last text message in favor of chatting with my teammate.

I glanced down the aisle at where she sat next to the

team doctor. She also refused to sit near me. I couldn't argue with that decision. If she was close, I'd want to touch her. I wouldn't maul her on the plane or anything, but if she was next to me, I'd want to hold her hand.

And even that was taking it too far. I sighed. Her job, not mine, would be in jeopardy if we were caught, and that wasn't okay. Nor did it seem fair. I would never ask her to give anything up to be with me. I wanted to make her life better, not be the reason she had to sacrifice. And the way she acted like a skittish rabbit anytime management was around would become an issue if it continued to happen.

But there was no easy fix. I could ask for a trade; my contract had a trade clause in it. But that would more than likely put us at least half a country apart, since I'd have no control over where they would trade me. The thought made my chest ache. Baseball season was long, so if we lived states apart, we'd get two months a year together. What we had might be new, but I already knew that wouldn't be enough for me.

How hard could it be to keep this hidden for a little longer? If we made it through the season, we could go from there. It would give us time to settle into the relationship before making any big decisions. My contract would be up at the end of the year, so I might be a free agent anyway. Then it wouldn't matter. I could try to get to New York or Buffalo, somewhere not too far. Maybe it wasn't worth the stress now. We'd just have to keep our distance when we were at work.

My blood pressure spiked when Bosco stopped and

leaned over the seat directly in front of her. He smirked and then said something that caused her to chuckle. Irritation flooded me. What the fuck was he doing making her laugh? The guy was a flirt. With his naturally highlighted hair and dimpled smile, he was always getting the girls, but I didn't remember him flirting with Aurora specifically before now. I gritted my teeth when he leaned farther into her space, and when she ran a hand along the side of his neck, it took everything in me to stay where I was instead of storming over there and throwing him to the floor.

What the hell?

I locked my jaw and gripped my armrests as Bosco finally headed toward me.

"Why were you talking to Aurora?" I stood in the aisle, stopping him before he could sit.

He tipped his head to the side, his brows pulled together. "Rory?"

I gave him a clipped nod, swallowing back a string of questions I wanted to interrogate him with.

"Oh," he said, sliding past me so he could sit in the seat next to mine. "I twisted my neck the other day." He rubbed at the spot between his neck and shoulder where Aurora had touched him. "I was telling her that it felt tight again. If it doesn't loosen up, it's going to affect my swing."

In my periphery, Aurora was heading our way, but I kept my head down. She headed past us to the back of the plane, and I did my best to pretend I didn't notice her presence. When she appeared next to me a moment later, though, it was impossible not to acknowledge her.

She held a heat patch up in front of her. "Can you get up so I can put this on Kyle's neck?"

"No. My head hurts," I said, rubbing at my temple. "Lean over me."

Her tight lips and cocked brow called me on my bullshit, but she didn't argue. As she leaned across me, I breathed in her floral scent and held it in my lungs. If that was as much of her as I could get, then I'd take it.

"Man, you're being a dick today," Kyle said as she adjusted the heat patch on his neck.

I shrugged. I liked her in my space, and being able to slide my finger along the exposed skin of her waist as her shirt rode up from stretching across me was worth the glare she gave me when she stood back up.

"Let me know how it feels when we land, Kyle," she said to Bosco. Then, with another quick glare at me, she turned and headed back to her seat.

"What'd you do to her?" Bosco frowned, looking from Aurora to me. "I think she hates you."

I chuckled. Maybe we had nothing to worry about after all.

16

Rory

"With that swing, you'd never know the kid was hurting." Beckett clapped as Mason swung. The sound of the bat cracking echoed off the walls. Then the ball was flying into the outfield between the center and right fielders.

"See how he almost cradles the arm against his body when he's running? That's how you know he's hurting worse than he's saying." Cortney leaned forward and frowned down at Mason, who'd stopped at second base.

We were leading the Dallas Stars, two to one. I'd been called up to the box, yet since I'd arrived two batters ago, neither of the men had acknowledged me.

I cleared my throat again, this time finally garnering Beckett's attention.

He swung around, his face set in his usual frown. "Oh good, you're here." Then he turned back to the field.

Wringing my hands, I waited. Yes, I was here. But was he going to tell me why they'd called for me?

"Cortney thinks we should be talking about IR again for the shoulder. But nothing in your report says that. What's he saying to you about it?"

"Uh." I glanced from him to Cortney, worrying my bottom lip. Mason had admitted more than once that it was sore, but he promised it wasn't serious. My exams weren't showing anything either. If they were, I would have suggested it immediately. "I—"

"She's not going to tell us anything." Without turning to face me, Cortney tightened the bun on the back of his head. "You are not where her loyalties lie. Trust me."

My heart stuttered at his words. Did Cortney know? About Mason and me? The way he'd looked at us in the training room the other day made me wonder, but he'd left it alone and hadn't brought it up again.

Nothing about my reports had been inaccurate, and I was hiding nothing for Mason. In the most recent one, I'd even acknowledged that neither he nor I felt that he was at 100 percent.

But did Cortney think I was hiding something? I swallowed and tried my best to keep my expression neutral, even though, on the inside, I was panicking.

"She works for us. We pay her. Why wouldn't she be loyal?" Beckett frowned at his GM before turning back to me. "What do you think?"

I shrugged. "Like I mentioned in my last report, I don't think his shoulder is 100 percent. But we play guys at 80 percent every day."

Beckett nodded and whacked Cortney's arm. "See? I told you."

"Was that it?" I asked.

"Just check him after the game." For the first time, Cortney turned and looked at me, and from his expression, the way he scrutinized me, it was clear he knew more than he was saying. "Email me a full report."

Stomach churning, I focused on breathing normally and nodded. Yes, I'd give him a full report. Because I wanted to keep my job.

"How does it feel?" I lifted Mason's arm, trying for a third time to help him stretch his shoulder.

He, on the other hand, was doing his best to keep me from doing my job.

"Can you lift your arm please? I need to see how tight it is."

He crossed his arms over his chest. "My shoulder is good enough. You didn't answer my question."

"Because I'm trying to do my job." I huffed. "Would you please cooperate?"

With his free hand, he grasped my waist, but I quickly stepped back and shot him a glare.

"I'm not trying to be an ass. I promise. I just miss you. I don't care what we do. I'll watch you read a book if that's what you want." He slumped and huffed out a defeated sigh. "But yeah. You can check my shoulder. Your job is the important thing here." Finally, he held his arm straight out in front of him.

The look he gave me was one of earnest intent. He really did care about my job, and he was doing his best to comply. But it was clear in his every move and expression, even if he hadn't told me repeatedly over the last two days, that he missed me.

And I missed him too. Just as much. I didn't want to treat him like I did every other athlete I worked with, but I had to. "How about we make a deal? If you're a good boy and let me finish checking out your shoulder without fighting or complaining, then I will."

He tipped his chin up and met my gaze, his eyes sparkling with a hope that had been missing since that day in the training room when Cortney had almost caught us.

And I couldn't fight my smile.

"Did you just tell him to be a good boy?"

My heart plummeted at the sound of Bosco's voice.

Chest aching and dread threatening to overtake me, I spun and found him standing in the doorway, only then realizing that we'd had that entire conversation with the door wide open.

17

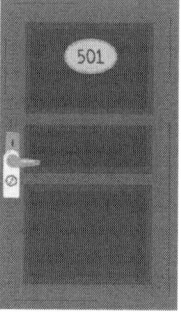

Mason

Shit. As much as I liked to joke around with Aurora, the last thing I wanted to do was get her in trouble. Yet here I was, messing with her within earshot of the guys.

"I'm just giving her a hard time." I hopped off the table and turned toward Aurora but kept my distance. "You get everything Miller wanted you to look at?"

She nodded, her cheeks pink and her gaze averted. "Uh...did you need me to check your neck?" she asked Bosco.

"No, I grabbed a heat pack from Doc." He thumbed over his shoulder. "I'll do that after I shower."

Perfect. I needed to do the same, so this would give me a good excuse to herd Bosco out of here. "I'm going that way too." I headed for the door, but as I stepped into the hall, I spun back to Aurora. "How about I check in before the game tomorrow so you can look at the inflammation and tape my shoulder?"

She nodded awkwardly but didn't speak, so I left it at that and hurried out of the room.

Bosco paused next to me. "Maybe I was wrong about her hating you, huh?"

I tamped down my frustration and gave him an easy shrug. My teammates would be cool about it if they knew. We'd all known about Chris and Avery long before Coach and management found out. But I didn't have the same faith in the training staff or the coaches, and I'd be damned if I said anything that put Aurora's job at risk.

"I probably need to stop giving her shit."

Kyle scoffed. "That'll be the day."

With a long breath out, I forced the tension in my shoulders to ease. That was true. That's who I was, and if I didn't at least mess with her a bit, then it'd be obvious something was up.

I shot her a text so she'd have my room number, then I hopped in the shower. The short message didn't warrant a response, but regardless, I was disappointed not to see one when I got out.

"Coming out to the bar?" Emerson asked as I pulled a Revs T-shirt over my head.

"Nah, my shoulder's bothering me," I said, rolling it out.

It wasn't any worse than any injury in the past, but I was frustrated about the way Miller was giving Aurora a hard time about it. He worried about everything, and I wasn't sure she realized that. Regardless of the severity, Miller would be all over her about my shoulder. That was a fact. The man couldn't help but stress.

He was also observant as fuck. And since he already

had us in his sights, we had to be extra careful around him. But until last year, he'd been my teammate, and he was the guy Dragon had gone to when he fell in love with Avery but had been told by her father that she was off-limits. And Miller had helped him out.

"Bothering ya, huh? Need to go back to Rory?" Bosco chuckled and cocked one brow. "Didn't you just tell her it was good?"

"It is. I mean it was." I pinched the bridge of my nose. "Look, I have a headache. Leave me alone."

"Uh-huh. Rory gonna help with that too?"

I dropped my hands to my sides and balled them into fists, homing in on Bosch. "Leave her *alone*."

Instead of clapping back, he stood there, his eyes running over me. He crossed his arms and rocked back on his heels, finally looking away.

"Fuck, you're almost as moody as Damiano now." Martinez shook his head, and the rest of the guys chuckled.

"I hate you all," Damiano mumbled. "I'm not going out either. Going back to the room and calling Avery."

"Then I'm definitely going out," Asher said. "I have no interest in sticking around for that *I love you more, no I love you more* shit."

"Keep Avery out of whatever this is." Damiano shot Asher a glare.

Coach Wilson strode by then, letting out a long sigh, and headed straight for the exit. He did his best to stay out of anything between Dragon and Avery. The man hated drama.

Despite the moodiness Martinez had commented on,

I couldn't help but laugh. I really did like these guys. Though Bosco was all of a sudden watching me a bit too knowingly. Like he might be just as clued in as I was beginning to think Miller was.

Dragon spent all of last season winning Avery over. He'd never kept his efforts a secret from us, so although we razzed him about it endlessly, we had his back and kept what we knew from Coach.

But this was different. The concern here wasn't that hooking up with Aurora would piss off Coach Wilson. No. The risk was to her job. So I had to be more diligent about keeping this under wraps. Even the guys couldn't know. Regardless of how much I trusted them, the more people who knew, the bigger the chance that someone would let a detail slip, and that would be it. If we could make it through the season without being discovered, then we'd figure out our next steps. But the one thing that was certain was that I wouldn't let her go.

By the time we got back to the hotel and I got Emerson out of the room, I was crawling out of my skin. Now she was almost half an hour late, and I was sitting on the edge of my mattress, my knee bouncing, holding my phone in my hand, telling myself not to send yet another text. When the knock finally echoed around the room, I sprang off the bed like a kangaroo and darted for the door.

"You're late." I tugged her into the room. As the door slammed, I pinned her against the wall and ran my nose up her neck, inhaling her scent. "Thought you might've changed your mind." Now that she was in my arms, the tension that had coiled so tight inside me eased. The sneaking around should be hot and fun, but keeping our relationship a secret was stressing me out. I constantly felt like I was on the edge of losing her.

She shook her head, raking her nails up my back. "Sorry, I had to go out to dinner with Anderson, Miller, and Langfield. They needed assurances, *again*, that you're okay."

With my face buried in the crook of her neck, I cupped her ass and lifted her.

"Although," she chuckled, "if they could see you now, then they would know the shoulder is fine."

I pressed my lips against hers, savoring the taste of her on my tongue, then carried her to the bed.

"Someone's in a hurry." She arched back and wiggled from side to side in my arms.

I pulled her close again. I hadn't had nearly enough of her, and I needed to feel her body pressed to mine. Heat consumed me as her soft breasts met the hard plane of my chest. I skated my lips down the soft skin of her neck, lost in her scent and her warmth, and when I pressed them into the hollow behind her ear, she shivered.

"You wouldn't see me last night." I nipped gently at her flesh. Fuck, I'd missed her. Being without her had left me with this itchy need to prove to myself that she was still mine.

"We're not going to be able to see each other every night."

I pulled away and scoffed. "Why not?" My heart hammered in my chest, and not just because I was turned on. No, suddenly, trepidation and frustration were threatening to take over. Was this not what she wanted?

Because being with her, totally, completely, was sure as shit what I was working toward.

"It's not realistic." She lowered her chin, letting her hair hide her face. "We either spend forever hiding this or one of us has to leave the Revs. And if that happens, there's a good chance one of us will have to move, and that scenario will come with its own set of problems."

My heart lurched as I took in the gorgeous woman below me. Fuck. Were those our only choices? To hide or to spend our days apart? No. There had to be a better solution, and one we could come up with soon.

"How about, for now, we put those thoughts aside and enjoy the moment?" she suggested, slipping her hands under my T-shirt.

I helped her pull the shirt over my head, then captured her lips again. "Hell, yes. I'll enjoy every moment I have with you. Nothing makes me happier than hearing you moan my name."

I cuffed the back of her neck and lowered my face to hers. I had no issue getting to be the one who gave her pleasure.

Soft, plush lips pressed against mine briefly before I ran my tongue along her bottom lip, coaxing her to open for me.

She opened her mouth, and with a groan, I sank into the kiss. But simply owning her mouth wasn't enough. I needed to dominate her. To prove that she was mine. That I could make her feel more than anyone else ever could. The slight moan that echoed deep in her chest only encouraged me.

My pulse pounded with anticipation as I skimmed a

hand down the soft skin of her neck. My dick throbbed against my zipper, begging for her.

She arched off the mattress into me. Full, round breasts pushed into my chest. God, I loved her tits. My hand skimmed the satin skin of her neck and shoulder, then drifted lower until I found the hem of her shirt. I needed less between us. I cupped her breast, her nipple hardening beneath the lace of her bra. One brush of my thumb over it, and she rewarded me with a breathy moan, causing a deep, hard ache in my cock. With a flick, I released the center clasp of her bra, freeing her tits.

I thrust against her, and her answering whimper vibrated through me. She might not see yet that this was meant to be, but with every touch, every breath, every smile, every whimpering moan, I was more certain this woman was my forever. I shifted slightly to lift her shirt over her head and tossed it to the side before I removed her black pants.

She lay against the white bedding in just a thin black thong, her tan skin smooth and inviting. Her big tits with dark pink nipples begged for my touch. She pressed her teeth into her bottom lip as her eyes begged for more. She was fucking stunning. She was fucking mine.

And she was going to realize that.

Her brown eyes scanned my face. "Mason?" she whispered.

"You. Are. Mine," I commanded. And although I meant it as a statement, she nodded as she slowly wet her lips.

"I'm yours, Mason, so touch me. Take me. Make us both feel good," she begged, arching up, trying to close the distance between us. I leaned down and ran my lips against the curve of her breast, and in response, goose bumps erupted along her skin.

Damn, I needed to feel her against me.

I yanked my shirt over my head, then dove in again and claimed her lips. Her soft skin rubbed against the plains of my chest as she wrapped her legs around my waist. With one hand, I jerked down my sweats, then I kicked them off.

She thrust up. "Mason."

The damp fabric of her thong rubbed rough against my boxers. My cock surged, desperate to break free and slam into her tight pussy. She rocked again. Fuck. She felt like heaven. She was wet and ready, but I wanted her begging for me.

The idea of the sweet plea leaving her mouth rocked through me. Slowly, I worked my way down her body until my lips ghosted over the thin lace of her thong.

"Damn, you're so wet." I groaned, inhaling the scent of her arousal.

"Yes, I need your mouth on me. I need you to touch me," she answered.

That desperate plea was music to my ears, and I rewarded her with a long, slow lap over her pussy. Her moan was all the encouragement I needed to continue.

Having her writhing under me was everything. Something I needed every day.

I sank two fingers deep inside her and curled them upward, searching for the spot that would leave her legs shaking. That would have her crying my name.

"Yes, right there." She moaned, writhing on the bed.

I flicked my tongue over her clit in rapid strokes until her pussy gripped me as she came, calling my name. My chest tightened and the feel of her pleasure coating my tongue. I needed more. I wanted to suck out every drop and then fill her back up with mine.

"Mine," I commanded.

Her blond hair was fanned out on the white sheet behind her head as she looked back at me. "Yes, I want to be yours. Make me yours, and you'll be mine," she whispered.

Her words settled deep inside me.

"I'll always be yours." With a long exhale, I guided myself inside her hot body. So wet and ready, she took every inch of me like she was made for it. I watched her body stretch to take me inside. Seeing us linked together made me burn with the need for more.

"Look at how we fit." I glanced back up and got lost in her deep brown eyes. As if she was looking into my soul and leaving her mark there. I'd never felt like this before.

"Please Mason. Move. I need you to move," she begged.

I held her there for the briefest moment, then pulled back and thrust hard. Her tits bounced below me with each thrust as she pushed against me, pulling me deeper. My lips sealed over hers, connecting us more as I rutted against her. Something inside me snapped, like a floodgate opening, and my emotions rushed over me. This was more than sex. This was more than pleasure. Her responding moans only spurred me on. Every pound was driving her higher. With every stroke, her pussy gripped my cock tighter.

"Come with me, baby," I demanded. "Let me feel that pussy gripping my cock. Let me own your pleasure, like you own me."

"Yes," she moaned, rocking harder against me.

My stomach tightened, and I thrust hard into her, losing control.

She clenched around me as her pussy milked my cock. My hips slammed forward faster and harder until I exploded.

"Mine," I growled. "Mine. Always."

Her eyes weren't open, but she looked blissed out, perfectly glowing below me. I leaned down and gently kissed her lips. I held her for one long second before I pulled myself out of her tight heat.

She sighed, and I helped her roll off the bed, knowing she needed the bathroom.

She stood beside the bed, her hair a mess in that just-fucked way and beard burn on her thighs that clearly marked her as mine, and headed for the bathroom.

My chest ached as I watched her go, the pain one I'd never experienced before. It was longing and need and fear and love all wrapped up together, and it only reinforced my need to find a solution to our issue.

I loved my team, and the game, and the fans. I liked the show of it. But none of it made me as happy as being with Aurora did. She needed to know that. Soon. In a few weeks, I'd have to make a move one way or another. And I needed her to be sure of me before I did something that could tear us apart.

18

Mason

A CLICK SOUNDED an instant before the door slammed against the deadbolt, startling me from where I'd dozed while waiting for Aurora to come back to bed.

Was she leaving? Without saying goodbye? What the fuck? I jackknifed to a sitting position and glared at the door, but Aurora was nowhere in sight.

"Why'd you lock me out?" Emerson called from the hallway.

Fuck. I jumped to my feet, and like a chicken with my head cut off, I ran around the bed in search of my clothes. Once I'd located my jeans, I stumbled around, pulling them up. My foot caught, and I teetered to one side. The mattress slowed my fall before I hit the floor.

"Dude, you okay?" Emerson banged on the door.

"Yeah, I got caught in the blanket." I winced the second the words were out, because the explanation was ridiculous. Except I'd seen Emerson do that exact thing this morning, so it wasn't unbelievable.

I pushed back to my feet, scooped up the rest of my clothes and Aurora's, and tucked them under the sheet piled on the bed, only to realize the twisted sheets and blankets screamed *sex bed*. So I stuffed them under one pillow, then quickly straightened the bedding. When I was finished, it looked like an eight-year-old had made the bed, but Emerson was banging again, so it would have to do.

"Whatcha you doing in there?"

Oh shit. I'd fixed the sex bed, but did it smell like sex in here too?

Heart pounding, I spun in a circle, looking for a way to fix that problem. I froze when I caught sight of the spray bottle on the dresser and lunged for it. Without hesitation, I hustled around the room, spraying Emerson's cologne, coughing as I went.

Fucking hell, this stuff was strong. But with any luck, it covered up the smell of sex lingering in the air.

"Are you purposely being an ass?" Emerson called, sounding annoyed, which was all wrong for the happy-go-lucky guy.

What the hell was going on? When the guys went out, Emerson always stayed out until well past two. He never had trouble finding women to flirt with and hang out with, and it was almost a guarantee that he'd still be there when the bar shut down for the night.

"Coming," I called. I stopped beside the bathroom door and murmured a "just keep it locked" to Aurora, hoping she could hear me, then forced myself to open the main door for Emerson.

When I did, I came face to face with a sight I'd never witnessed before. Emerson looked almost *sad*. Though I couldn't be sure. I didn't think he had ever experienced that emotion. Happy and goofy were his defaults.

"Why are you back so early?" I forced myself not to look at the door behind me.

"Eh, wasn't feeling it." He shrugged, but as he did, he froze. Then he lifted his nose and sniffed the air.

As he turned in a full circle, still sniffing, my heart pounded, but I kept my expression even and fisted my hands at my sides to steady them.

"Why were you spraying my cologne? Did you take a massive shit or something? Why bother wasting it? You've done that plenty of times, and you never cared that I gag."

For the love of God. I pinched my brow, praying Aurora hadn't heard that.

He sniffed again and cocked a brow. "Weed?"

"No, I just..." *What the fuck, Mason?* How was I going to explain this? "I just like the smell." I shrugged and quickly changed the subject back to him. "But what do you mean you weren't feeling it?" I asked, raising my voice in hopes that Aurora could hear us and be clued in to what was going on, yet still hoping she'd missed the one about the big shit. "You're always out."

"What's the matter with you?" Emerson stepped around me. "Why do you care if I'm here or not?"

On any other day, I wouldn't. But Aurora was naked

in the bathroom, so he had to go. "I'm worried about you."

He tipped his head to the side, making his wavy hair flop over his forehead. "Me?" He pointed to his chest. "I'm fine. I'm just gonna take a shower and go to bed."

"No," I blurted out, my heart lurching. "You can't take a shower."

"What?" He peered around me and narrowed his eyes at the closed bathroom door.

"It's just ..." I opened my arms wide. "I need a hug."

Emerson was the hugger of the group. There was no way he'd turn me down. But it would only buy me a minute. I had to figure out how to get rid of him.

"You want a hug?" His expression morphed from slightly annoyed to relaxed. "Aw, bring it in."

I awkwardly patted his back as I went through my options. And when he pulled back, I did the only thing that made sense. I rubbed my shoulder.

"You're hurting?" His eyes went wide. Bingo. Of course he'd be worried. The whole team had been stressing about it all freaking week.

"Yeah, it's just sore." I hunched over and stretched my good arm back farther, exaggerating the struggle of finding the right spot and rubbing at it. "I just don't want them to pull me."

"Dude, none of us wants that. Potter can't hit for shit. Want me to go get Rory?"

"Yeah," I said, keeping my tone even. "Could you find her for me?"

With a nod, he spun, tripping over his own feet, then headed out the door.

The second the door was shut behind him, Aurora stepped out of the bathroom, wrapped in a white towel. "How is he going to find me?"

"Since you're here, searching for you will keep him busy for a while. And it was the only way I could get him out of the room." Heart still beating a bit too hard in my chest, I wrapped my arms around her.

She sighed against my chest, and just like I knew she would, she tried to throw up walls.

"We're not doing this again. I almost had a heart attack." Her voice cracked on the last word.

Fuck. I felt like an ass.

"I know, babe. We can just hang out at home."

With another defeated sigh, she nodded and stepped out of my hold. "Where are my clothes? Apparently, I need to head out so Emerson can find me."

I pulled the pillow back to reveal them, and she dressed quickly. After she'd finger combed her hair and I'd stolen another kiss, I cracked the door and peeked out into the hallway. When the coast was clear, I ushered her out. As the door to the stairwell slammed behind her, I slumped, rubbing at the ache in my chest. Damn. This whole situation stunk. With a defeated sigh, I flopped onto the bed and threw my good arm over my eyes.

Two minutes later, the door opened again. "Sorry, man, I went by her room." Emerson shrugged. "She must be out with someone."

I held back a smirk. She'd definitely been with someone. But I couldn't tell him that I was that someone. And damn, I hated that.

"I mean, objectively, she's hot."

I locked my jaw and tried my best not to glare at him.

"What?" he asked, clearly reading into my silence incorrectly. "You didn't notice that? You were with her for a whole week."

"I'd be blind not to notice." I tried to keep the growl out of my voice. "Did you want a shower?"

He studied me, his brows pulled together, but after a moment, he shook his head. "You sure are acting weird tonight."

I blew out a breath. "Yeah, man. I just need a good night's sleep."

Because it was going to be a long four days on the road if I could only see her from a distance.

19

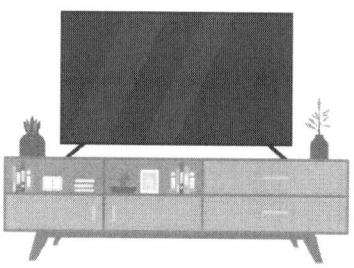

Rory

I SNUGGLED BACK into the solid body behind me and relished the way the heat of him enveloped me. Cuddled on the sofa with Mason was my new favorite place to be. We'd been back in Boston for five days, and we had another two to spend together before he left again. We'd spent all but a night or two at his place, because relaxing on his sofa in his arms with a blanket draped over us, watching our favorite show, was nothing short of perfect.

"It's fucking annoying how long it took Booth to admit how he felt." I couldn't see Mason's face, but I could tell by the tone of his voice that he was glaring at the TV. "Man up already."

"Really?" I chuckled, rolling to my back so I could tease him. "So if you liked somebody, you'd tell them right away? Cause I remember—"

He mussed my hair and dropped a kiss to the tip of my nose. "Hey, don't give me shit. I was seventeen. And you were way out of my league."

I rolled my eyes but leaned into him. "Oh, please."

In one fluid movement, he pushed up and hovered over me.

"You were and still are so far out of my league," he said, his green eyes full of intense honesty and a hint of fear. "And it stresses me out to know that at any moment, you might realize it."

Heat crept up my neck and into my face at his honest—though off-base—admission.

Shifting so he was balanced on his good arm, he cupped my cheek. "I was an idiot back then. This time, I made my intentions clear pretty quickly, didn't I? It was what, three days before I locked you up?"

A nervous laugh escaped me, because although he wasn't wrong… "I guess." With everything between us, it was hard to call us together. Even if part of me wanted to be.

Any trace of lightness in his expression vanished at my words, and suddenly, he was glowering at me. "We have issues to deal with, Aurora. But don't think that means I'm not 100 percent invested in this. In us."

My heart skipped at the sincerity that laced every word. I felt the same way, and I wanted, more than anything, to believe we had a future. But it was hard to picture it with the way things were right now. "I know it's just…"

I was at a loss for how to put my fears into words. Because I'd been running myself ragged, mentally working through every scenario, and the only solution I had come up with was one I wasn't sure I'd be okay with. In order to be with Mason and stay in Boston, I'd have to quit my job. I could work at a rehab facility locally. Or maybe even a hospital. If it meant I could have Mason too, it was worth considering. But this solution meant giving up one dream for another. Because Mason had firmly cemented himself in that category. A real relationship with him was now a dream. It had only been a couple of weeks, but we'd picked up right where we left off eleven years ago. Like no time had passed. And it was easy to admit, to myself at least, that I wanted this feeling, this man, forever.

"Just be here with me." He kissed me quickly, then pushed to his feet and headed for the kitchen.

As he went, my stomach twisted itself into knots. Had I upset him? The thought had just taken hold when he appeared again, carrying a bottle of my favorite flavor of sparkling water. Relief washed over me, and I couldn't stop the smile that spread across my face. He always knew when I needed something, and he paid attention to the little things. Keeping my favorite brand and flavored water in his fridge might not seem like much, but it was just one of many, many things he did to show he cared, and the thought he put into making me feel appreciated still floored me.

I sat up, and he dropped onto the cushion beside me and pulled me close. As I rested my head on his good shoulder, he threaded his fingers through my hair, instantly banishing all my worries.

A contented sigh escaped me. It was nice to be here

together. Although we saw each other at the stadium all week, we had to act indifferent toward each other, and I hated it. We both did. But when he pressed his lips against my temple, my body sagged, and a future with him didn't feel hopeless. It felt perfect.

20

Rory

"Are you crazy?" My chest tightened at the thought. I could not have heard him correctly. "We can't go *out* to dinner."

For the last few weeks, we'd spent every night he was in Boston together, but we'd stayed at either his place or mine.

"I'll wear a hat." He shrugged. "No one will recognize us, and as of today, it's been two months since you let me kiss you again. I want to take you somewhere nice. Spoil you."

My heart stuttered, and all my arguments escaped me. I'd had no idea it was a special day, but of course, he did. And I'd never had anyone make a big deal of something as silly as a two-month anniversary of the day he kissed me. Hell, the guy I dated for almost two years forgot our one-year anniversary.

Mason looped his arms around my waist and tucked

me into his chest. "What's the point of being a rich baseball player if I can't even spoil my girl with dinner on our anniversary?"

This man. I swallowed back the emotion threatening to overtake me. Because no matter how much I longed to experience life with him outside the walls of our apartments, I couldn't. Not yet. "They see you in a hat all the time," I finally mumbled, because it was the easiest response.

"It sounds strange, but when I'm out in Boston wearing a hat, they don't see Mason Dumpty." He chuckled against my ear. The sound and the way it vibrated through us both sent a shiver down my spine. "So what do you say? Can I take my girl to dinner?"

"Mason." My whole being ached with the urge to say yes. This man made it so hard to say no. "We can't. I'll get fired if they find out. It's my job on the line, not yours."

He slumped in my arms, and with a sigh into my hair, he pressed his lips against my forehead. "Sorry. You're right. I'm not being fair. I'll DoorDash something for dinner."

The way his shoulders sagged with disappointment when he pulled back a little made my heart splinter. More than anything, I wanted to go out to dinner with him. I wanted to do all the things normal couples did. But it wasn't realistic. At least right now.

"It's not that I don't want to..." I ran my fingers down his arm, hoping he sensed my sincerity.

"I know, babe. It's fine." He shrugged.

Banging on the front door had my heart leaping into my throat.

Mason himself practically jumped out of his skin. "Who the fuck is that?" Frowning, he released his hold on me and strode for the door.

He hunched low so he could check the peephole, and when he turned back, his eyes were wide. "It's the guys," he mouthed.

Shit. We'd been so careful to avoid each other at work. And Mason was sure no one suspected anything, but if I didn't get out of here, they'd all know the truth. I spun in a circle, searching for a place to hide.

Mason pushed me toward the coat closet and shoved the coats aside, making room. "Stay here. I'll get rid of them."

I stepped in and shouldered my way between his coats and the wall. When I turned to face Mason, he was frowning. Neither of us spoke, and when his friends pounded on the door again, he shut the door between us, blotting out the light.

My heart sank to my stomach as I rested my head against the cold wooden door. We really couldn't keep doing this. I was an almost thirty-year-old, hiding like a teenager. Maybe it was time to accept that I'd have to give up my job. Although disappointment washed over me every time I considered it, the idea of not being with Mason was so much harsher, like a lancing pain in my chest. I couldn't give him up.

The brush of the weather seal against Mason's wooden floors was barely audible when he finally opened the door to the guys.

"Dude, when did you get so slow?" I was pretty sure that was Emerson.

"It's like he crawls to the door." Hmm, was that Asher Price?

The next comment was likely from Kyle, and it had my stomach twisting. "Bet if it was one of his hookups, he'd get his ass in gear."

Mason growled. "I don't have hookups."

"Exactly. We've left you alone since you've been dealing with the head shit, but it's time to come out and rejoin the land of the living." That was definitely Emerson.

I held my breath as footsteps echoed and the voices moved deeper into the apartment.

"Wren and Jana are coming. Maybe you can finally tap that." That was definitely Kyle. "You've been sniffing around Jana forever."

Uck. The twisting turned to rolling at the image that popped into my head. I had no idea who Jana was, but suddenly, I hated the woman.

A loud bang reverberated through the floor, making me jump. "I have no interest in her."

My lips pulled up in a smile. I couldn't say that didn't make me feel good.

"Stop saying that shit, Streaks. I am never hooking up with anyone again. I've been telling you that for fucking weeks, so back the fuck off."

My heart ached at the anger in Mason's voice, and I wished more than anything that I could be out there with him, soothing his frustration.

"Jeez, dude. Chill out. Between you and Dragon, it's like fire everywhere lately." The chuckle Emerson let out was strained. "Although I wouldn't break shit over it. I'm not looking to hook up either, so let's go out and have fun. Leave it at that."

"Either way, we're not taking no for an answer," Kyle said. "It's our only off night. We need to let off steam."

"No." Mason's tone was clipped. "I'm not feeling it."

"That sounds like bullshit to me. You've been so tense lately. If anyone needs a night out to relax, it's you."

"Why aren't you with your family, Price? Figured you'd spend all the time with them you could before we head out on the road again."

"They're in California, since it's the kids' break from school. Kylie's set on taking up some work again. Apparently, the kids and I aren't enough for her anymore. She needs something to give her *fulfillment*." Asher Price spent most of his off time with his wife and kids, but his wife was a former Hollywood fixer. She'd handled bad press for the big names until she married Asher. Without seeing him, it was hard to tell whether he was supportive of his wife's decision. Knowing him, though, I was sure he must be a million percent behind her.

A thud and a grunt came from the other side of the door, startling me from my thoughts and putting me on guard.

"Jesus, Bambi. Are you already drunk?" Mason said.

"No, why?"

I bit back a chuckle, but as the doorknob turned, my heart launched itself into my throat. No. No, no, no. This was not happening.

"I'm grabbing your coat, and you're coming out with us for a drink. If you want to leave after one, then fine, but we won't take no for an answer."

"Streaks, don't—"

The door swung open, and light flooded the space. I blinked, and when my vision came into focus again, all I could see was Kyle's wide-eyed stare.

"Oh, fuck me." His lips turned down into a frown, then he slammed the door, and I was thrown into darkness once again.

"You know what? I bet it's the shoulder again, and he just doesn't want to tell us."

Mason cleared his throat. "Fine. Yeah, it's tight and I'm cranky."

"Aw, do you need a hug?" Emerson asked. "Bring it in."

Price chuckled.

"You know who could help rub that out for you…?" Kyle started.

Wincing, I clutched my hands to my chest.

"Fuck off," Mason growled.

"Want me to call her? I have her number."

Shit. My phone was out there somewhere. If Emerson called, things would get so much worse. Mason and Kyle were close. There was a good chance we could convince him to keep this quiet. But if others found out and word spread? Dammit.

I pulled in a deep breath, waiting for the sound of my ringtone, only to remember that I'd shoved my phone into my pocket. With a relieved exhale, I pulled out the phone to silence it, but as I did, it slipped through my fingers and clattered to the floor.

My heart stopped, along with all sounds on the other side of the door. I swallowed down the tears threatening to take over and wrapped my arms around myself, bracing for another one of his friends to tear open the door and discover me.

"What was that?" Price finally asked.

"Rats," Mason said.

I shut my eyes and breathed through my panic. Not one of them would believe that Mason's high-end penthouse had rats.

"No way you have rats." See? Even Emerson didn't buy it.

"No. Cats," Mason corrected.

"You have a cat?" Price asked.

Kyle only chuckled. At least he wasn't making the situation worse by calling us out.

"No, neighbor's cats. They come through the vents."

Price scoffed. "Why don't you do something about that shit?"

"I love cats. Can I see them?" Emerson's footsteps moved closer at an alarming speed, and my heart rate picked up right along with them.

"No!" Mason called. "They bite. Vicious little things. Don't open the door."

The solid wood door rattled in front of me as something slammed into it.

"You let vicious cats into your apartment?" I could picture Emerson's face at the words. Head cocked to the side, eyes wide.

"That's why I lock them in the closet."

Kyle laughed. "Okay, guys. I think Mason needs some time alone with his…kitten."

Mortified, I dropped my head into my hands and silently whimpered.

"Let's get out of here."

After some grumbling, the front door opened and shut again.

A moment later, the door swung open, and I stepped out. "So Kyle knows."

Mason nodded. "I'm not worried about him. He's not going to tell anyone."

I blew out a breath. "We can't keep doing this."

"I know."

"So what do we do?"

He pulled me into his arms and rested his chin on top of my head. "I don't know, but we'll figure it out."

I sagged against him and gave in to the tears. I wanted so badly to believe him.

21

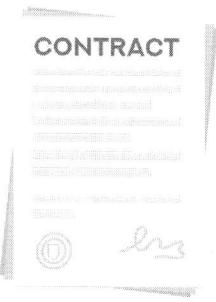

Mason

"You want what?" Beckett bit out as he narrowed his eyes at me.

To him, I supposed my request seemed like it had come from out of the blue, but I'd been considering this option for weeks. My contract included a trade clause, thank fuck, because this was the best solution I could come up with. After the other night, when Kyle discovered Aurora at my place and the other guys almost had too, that became apparent. I wanted to keep playing baseball, but I wanted Aurora in my life more. So it was time to make my priorities clear. But in order for this to work, I needed to stay on the East Coast, and this needed to happen before the trade deadline.

"A trade?" Cortney asked, his demeanor and his expression much more calm.

"Yeah. I'm willing to go to Montreal, Buffalo, New York, DC, Pittsburg—"

Cortney cleared his throat and sat up straighter on the other side of his desk. "So you're staying within a radius of Boston?"

I nodded once. "As close as possible."

"What the duck is going on?" Beckett asked, scooting to the edge of his seat. "Is it Wilson? Or one of the other players?"

Cortney waved him off. "Relax."

"We are not letting our top guy go," Beckett growled. "We can fix this, Dumpty. What's the issue?"

With a frown, Cortney steepled his fingers and assessed me. "I think the better question is: Why do you want to stay near Boston? Do you have a specific reason?"

Forcing my shoulders back, I blew out a breath. It was time to confess. I took a breath—

"Wait." Beckett slapped the desk and eyed Cortney. "Like a *female* reason?"

The GM sighed. "What did we say about matchmaking?"

"That I'm the best at it." Beckett smirked.

"No one says that."

"Who is she?" The owner of the Revs, who was acting far too giddy at the prospect of a woman being my problem here, scrutinized me with the kind of intensity that immediately had me breaking into a sweat.

Cortney just sat back and raised one eyebrow.

I had no interest in a matchmaker. Things with Aurora and I would be fine as soon as we no longer worked for the same team.

"It doesn't matter. I just need a trade."

"It does matter. Give us a chance to move her."

"Absolutely not." I pushed to my feet and slammed both hands onto the desk. "That's the whole point." I whirled on Cortney. "She's wanted to be a trainer for a professional team since we were in high school. I won't be the one to mess that up for her."

Cortney kept his mouth shut and turned to Beckett.

When neither of them responded, I continued.

"I'll quit if I need to," I warned. "Fine me. Make me buy back my contract. Sue me. I don't care."

"A trainer?" Brows pulled low, Beckett scanned the room, as if he was mentally flipping through our staff list. With a tap of his fingers on the desk, his eyes went wide. "Rory?"

Cortney nodded before I had a chance to decide whether I wanted to confirm or deny her identity.

"Did he come to you again?" Beckett demanded, his jaw clenched tight.

"No, but I saw it." Cortney sighed. "I tried to subtly get them to come to me for help with the issue, but neither of them did. Now that you know that *we* know, can we clear the air?"

I shouldn't have been surprised. The man had dominated the plate for years because he paid attention to the minute details that everyone else missed.

I slumped back into my seat and roughed a hand down my face.

"Wait." Beckett sat up tall in his seat. "I can fix this. Easy."

"We are not moving her," I gritted out.

"Hold on." Beckett held out a hand. "She applied for a

position with the Bolts first. Let's just move her there. Those assholes are always hurt, so we have space to carry another trainer."

"That's what I was going to suggest." Cortney smirked. "But apparently, we can't move her."

"Move her to the Bolts?" That might be the best option we had. I wouldn't have to leave Boston, and she wouldn't either. She'd still have a job. But it wouldn't be the same job. And I wasn't sure she'd be okay with it. "I'm not making this decision for her."

Worry worked its way through me, coiling my muscles tight. Would she be pissed? I promised her that she wouldn't lose her job.

"Go get her," Beckett said. "We can't just leave it as it is now that it's out in the open."

Right. I swallowed past the lump in my throat. I'd get her, and hopefully she wouldn't be pissed.

22

Rory

I turned at the sound of the door cracking open.

"You busy, baby?" Mason stepped in, wearing a tight-lipped expression that immediately put me on edge.

Before I could get a single word out, my breathing had picked up. I had to know. "What's wrong?"

He swallowed and rocked back on his heels. "Langfield and Miller want to talk to us."

I brought my hands to my mouth and willed myself not to dissolve into tears. "Oh my God. Did Kyle say something?" My heart pounded and blood whooshed in my ears. Were they angry? Would they fire me today? God, I hoped they wouldn't yell.

"No." His tone was resolute, but his tight expression and the way he crossed his arms over his chest did nothing to ease my fears. "I told you Kyle would never say anything. They just want to talk." He tipped his head toward the hallway.

Forcing one foot in front of the other, I moved toward the door on shaky legs. "About what?" I wrung my hands as I passed him.

His shoulder hadn't been an issue in almost two weeks, so it wasn't that. Could it be—

"I asked for a trade."

I stopped mid-step, and he pulled up short behind me to keep from crashing into me. "You what?" Turning so we were face to face, I studied him, searching for any sign that he was joking.

He gently grasped my arms and spun me around, then placed a hand on the small of my back and urged me forward again. "I asked for an east coast trade." He repeated the words, but they didn't compute. A trade?

He hit the button for the elevator and stepped in closer than he should since we were at work.

He was leaving Boston? My stomach sank.

"Why?" I breathed, my heart crumbling into pieces. "What does that mean for us?"

The elevator doors slid open, and he pushed me inside. Once they were shut behind us, he turned me to face him. "I don't want you to be just my trainer." He pinched my chin between his thumb and finger, forcing me to look at him. "You're great at what you do, Aurora. But after I got hurt, rather than putting my head together again, you put my heart together again. Life was good before, but now it's amazing. All because of you. I didn't know what was missing until you came back into my life."

I tipped forward into his embrace.

"I'm done hiding this." He pressed his lips to the top of my head. "I love you, and I want the world to know."

My heart tripped at his words. Wide-eyed, I pulled back and took him in. He just looked down at me, wearing a small smile.

The pieces of my heart that had only just broken were already stitching themselves back together again. "I love you too."

He dropped his lips to mine, and we stayed like that, without taking it any further, until the elevator doors opened.

He pulled back and rubbed his hands up and down my arms. "This will be fine. I promise."

I nodded, but the lump that had lodged itself in my throat when Mason came to get me was still there. Because I still didn't see an easy solution.

When we stepped into the office, the first thing I saw was Beckett, who was pacing along the windows.

"Have a seat." Cortney waved to the pair of guest chairs.

I wasn't sure whose office this was. Though he was sitting behind the desk, and I could have sworn the nameplate on the door had read *Cortney Miller*, a huge Langfield jersey hung on the wall. The shelves filled with books again made it feel more like the office belonged to Cortney than Beckett...I glanced at the jersey again.

Mason directed me into one chair, then he took the seat next to me and squeezed my hand, grabbing my attention. "It's fine."

I nodded.

"Is this team—the Revs—the only team you're interested in working for?"

I swung my head up toward Beckett, who now stood still, his intense gaze on me.

Of course that was the first question. Because in the end, they were not going to move him. They'd rather move me. I let out a deep sigh.

"If she doesn't want to move, then we're doing it. You're trading me." Mason's glare was filled with so much heat I swore the temperature in the room shot up. Without taking his eyes off Beckett, he yanked me out of the chair and pulled me to him. "I told you this already. Eleven years ago, I was a fucking moron. I didn't fight hard enough, and I let shit get in the way. Because of that, I lost her. But this time? That. Is. Not. Happening." He was practically vibrating with anger as he pulled me onto his lap and held me tight.

This was the furthest thing from professional decorum, but I didn't have it in me to stop him. It didn't matter anyway. There was no way they'd let him go, so they were likely ready to give me my walking papers, regardless of whether I was sitting primly in a chair or draped over my boyfriend's lap.

"I will fight for her, and I'll spend every day doing what I can to make her life better. She will give up nothing for me. Ever. Respect that, or I swear to God, I will buy out my contract and walk away from baseball."

That statement hit me like a physical blow. But at the same time, it sent butterflies flitting through my body. Because that might have been the sweetest thing I'd ever heard.

His next words were a whisper against my ear. "You are my priority here. Do what makes you happy. That's all that matters to me."

I loved him for that. But he also mattered.

"What a grand gesture." Beckett smiled. "I love that."

Cortney rolled his eyes. "Mason, Rory applied for a position with the Bolts. When that was filled and we offered her a job with the Revs, she took it. So could we maybe have a conversation before you make this decision for her?"

"What?" Mason's arms tightened around me.

I nodded and pulled back as far as I could, though he didn't loosen his hold. "I did. I always wanted to work with hockey players." I turned back to the other men in the room. "Are you asking if I would transfer to the Bolts?"

Cortney cleared his throat. "We can't have you both on the same team, so we thought…"

"We allow fraternization to a certain point. How could we not? My wife works for me. And I lived with this idiot"—Beckett jerked a thumb toward Cortney—"for almost a year. But you can't be his trainer." He nodded at Mason. "Hockey players, though, they get hit in the head all the time. They could use all the help they can get."

"You want me to work for the Bolts?" My mind whirled. Seriously? I almost couldn't believe it.

"Is that what you want?" Mason turned me to face him.

There was no stopping the smile that split my face.

"That's what I've always wanted, to work for a hockey team. I would love that."

He ducked, surveying me closely. "Are you sure?"

"Absolutely." I nodded.

He turned back to face Cortney and Beckett. "Then there's no issue with us being together? Because she's moving in with me."

All the air left my lungs. "*What?*" We'd never even talked about moving in together.

His eyes were so full of love when they met mine. "Maybe not today. But eventually, yes, you're moving in with me. Then I'll propose, and then we're gonna get married and have five kids."

I was still processing his ridiculous statements when he addressed Cortney again. "So is that all okay, even if she works for the Bolts?"

This man. I couldn't hold back the laugh that bubbled out of me. He was being ridiculous, but he was adorably ridiculous.

"I don't have a problem with it. I love love." Beckett smiled, his chest puffed out proudly. "See? My matchmaking skills have come in handy again."

Cortney sighed and hung his head. "Yeah, Beckett."

"You, Shay, Delia, Avery…"

"Not sure how you get credit for Avery—"

"Oh, come on. It was all because of me."

"Actually," Mason chimed in, "pretty sure it was because of Puff."

"*Anyway.*" Cortney shook his head. "We're all good. We'll have you sign some paperwork, and then we'll get everything transferred over and have you start..." Cortney glanced up at Beckett.

"Next week," Beckett said, slipping his hands into his pockets.

Cortney made a choking sound in response.

Beckett shot him a disapproving look. "Why couldn't she start next week?"

"Shouldn't you check with your brothers?" Cortney prompted.

"No. I don't ask for their permission." Beckett shrugged. "I'll get everything taken care of."

"See?" Mason whispered against my ear. "I told you I would make it happen."

Maybe. Or maybe, all along, we were meant to be back together again.

Epilogue

Rory

"Did you really skate headfirst into the glass? Like no one pushed you?" I stood in front of Aiden Langfield, the center for the Bolts, as he turned his head slowly from one side to the other, careful not to go too fast. The team doctor had already assessed him for a concussion and determined that it was mild, but he could still play. Hockey players were crazy like that. I just needed to make sure he hadn't injured anything in his neck or shoulders when he went full-on into the glass of his own accord. And not even during the game.

He shrugged. "Shit happens."

Everyone joked that nothing bothered Aiden. And injury was nothing new to the man. Beckett was right when he said these guys hit their heads all the damn time. Between that and their neck and shoulder issues from the constant stick work, they kept me busy. But I'd loved the transition to the Bolts. The sound of the door opening caught my attention, and I turned to see Beckett step into the small training room, crossing his arms as he stared at his little brother.

"Doc says you have a mild concussion. You can't stay alone and Jill's out of town. We need to find someone for you to stay with to monitor it." He looked at me like I had the answer to that problem.

Oh no. Although Mason's concussion did bring us back together again, babysitting another professional sports player was not on my to-do list. And Mason's season had just ended, so I was enjoying us both being home together every night.

"Good thing there are so many of you Langfields." Surely one of Aiden's four siblings could babysit.

"Yeah, I'll put him with Gavin." Beckett smirked at the idea of pawning off his baby brother on a different sibling. "He'll love that."

I wasn't even going to ask if he planned to ask his permission. Beckett never asked anyone but his wife Liv about anything.

After I finished checking over Aiden, I made my way back up to the suite where my parents, Mason, and a few of the guys from the Revs were watching the game. Mason, being his usual over-the-top self, had bought season tickets at Bolts Arena so he and my parents could attend any games they wanted. And he'd made sure to make it to some around his baseball schedule already.

The minute I stepped inside the room, Mason pulled me into his arms and pressed his lips to my forehead. "How's Langfield?" he mumbled against my skin.

"Fine. Apparently, he just skated into the wall."

He chuckled. "Yeah, he was staring across the ice and just ran headfirst into the glass. Dude was in a trance."

"Not nearly as good as your stories of amazing flying catches. Like our personal super jet." Emerson put his arms out and mimicked an airplane soaring around. He only made it about three steps before he crashed into the half wall and teetered. His girl grabbed his shirt and yanked him so he didn't fall out the open window. Those two were definitely a pair. Black cat and golden retriever all the way.

Mason draped his arm around my shoulders. Regardless of whether it had been minutes, hours, or days, any time we were reunited, he was quick to pull me into his side. Even at home. It wasn't surprising that we were already living together.

Within weeks of my move to the Bolts, Mason had me spending most nights with him when he was in town. We were both busy, and neither of us got home before ten on game days, so by the end of August, I gave in to his begging and officially made his place *our* place.

"At least we don't have to worry about you getting hurt for a few months."

Mason shook his head.

"Speaking of hurt, how's our center doing?" My dad looked up from where he sat at the counter that lined the front of the suite. The first time my dad watched a game from up here, he was like a little kid. It was a preseason game, but he acted like it was the Super Bowl.

"Langfield's okay. Just a mild concussion. They're letting him play."

He nodded, humming thoughtfully at the news. I

wasn't surprised. Aiden was one of our best players, and if we had any shot at the cup this year, we couldn't afford to lose him.

"Hopefully the Bolts' season ends better than ours did." Mason settled on the stool by my dad and pulled me to stand between his thighs.

I glanced up at him. "I'm still surprised you all are taking the playoff loss so well."

He shrugged a shoulder. "There's always next season. And now I get to be home with you."

Although the night that ended their season had been intense, since then, all the guys seemed to be settling into the offseason and were happy to spend more time with their families.

"Avery and Damiano can focus on planning their wedding now." He nodded across the room to where the couple was chatting, totally engrossed in one another.

"You guys are going to be next, right?" Dad frowned at Mason. He didn't love the fact that we'd moved in together with no plan, but I didn't need marriage to know Mason was my future. We'd get there eventually.

"Nope." Emerson jumped in and wrapped his arm around his girlfriend, tucking her into his side. "I'm definitely next."

"No you're not." She pushed him away and whacked him in the stomach.

"I warned you when we moved in together that this was the next step." He laughed, not at all fazed by her death glare. "I'm not gonna keep stealing free milk."

"Jesus," Damiano muttered.

Mason's chuckle echoed against my ear. "I love these assholes almost as much as I love you."

I couldn't fight my smile.

"Fair warning, Humpty," Mason said, "we're definitely next. Gotta make sure Humpty Dumpty stays together for the rest of forever."

ALSO BY GRACIE YORK
AJ RANNEY & JENNI BARA

Gracie York Books:
Goldilocks and the Grumpy Bear
Tumbling Head Over Heels
Along Came The Girl
Peter Pumpkined Out

Jenni Bara Books:
More Than The Game
More Than Fine
More Than A Hero
More Than A Story
More Than Myself
Mother Maker
The Fall Out

AJ Ranney Books:
Always Yours
Wishing to be Yours
Impossibly Yours
Imperfectly Yours

A NOTE FROM THE AUTHORS

Dear Reader,

Thank you so much for continuing on this retelling journey with us. Humpty Dumpty was a tricky one to figure out but when Jenni started with the Boston Revs, Mason just appeared screaming to get knocked out. So we obliged him. We hope you loved him and Rory as much as we did. And all the fun easter eggs from Mother Maker and The Fall Out.

If you missed out on the Boston Revs world definitely start the Momcoms today with Mother Faker because you WILL NOT be disappointed with these four women living together in a falling down Boston brownstone.

If this is your first Gracie nursery rhythm you MUST go back and meet Goldilocks in Goldilocks and the Grumpy Bear. Jack in Tumbling Head Over Heels. Little

A NOTE FROM THE AUTHORS

Miss Muffet in Along came the Girl. And Pete in Peter Pumpkined Out. It's always fun finding new creative ways to retell these old favorites.

Where will we go next? Who knows.

Jenni and AJ

ACKNOWLEDGMENTS

Thank you to our wonderful readers, whose love for our characters and our books sometimes even outweighs our own. To our street and ARC teams, a big thank you for all your sharing, your reviews, your support, your shout-outs, your reels, your tiktoks, and your excitement for our stories. You are all the best!

Thank you to our families for all your support and love. We couldn't do this without you!

Beth, thank you for being so flexible and understanding with this book and everything. We are so glad we found you, and we will never stop singing your praises from the rooftop. You are amazing with your edits and proofreads and checking everything twice! You are thoughtful and detailed and amazing at keeping an author's voice. More than that, you are a friend who Jenni is so grateful to have in her life. Thank you for being the wonderful person you are.

Sara, as always, Jenni couldn't do this without you. Ten million conversations, a zillion favors, one more graphic, and the constant reminders that our good days start tomorrow. Your creativity also amazes me, and others since you constantly inspire people. Better than that you are an amazing friend and a wonderful caring person.

Jess, Jenni can't stop being grateful to Britt for dragging you to Salem with us! Because she got a friend and a champion out of the deal! You're 100 percent invested in Jenni's ball bunnies and that's something she couldn't do without. You are amazing and don't forget it.

Britt thank you for once again sharing Beckett, he is Jenni's favorite and she loves to have him come visit every one of her characters. You are amazing for letting us into your Boston sports world. If you haven't already check out both the Momcoms and the Revenge Games to meet all of Britt's amazing book boyfriends.

Daphne, thank you for a being friend and teacher. The amount of knowledge and insight you have given is something that we are eternally grateful for. And your friendship is something we don't want to do without. Everyone should check out the Lovewell Lumberjacks because if you don't know these plaid wearing ax swinging guys yet you are missing out.

And thank you, Amy Jo, for not only beta reading and running our teams, but for all the beautiful book minis, bookmarks, and other swag you've made for us. Plus all you do to help us market our books on Tiktok.

To all our author friends and beta readers, thank you for being supportive and inspiring writers. Kristin Lee, Alexandra Hale, Lo Evertt, Julia Jarett, Amanda Zook, JL Reed, Garry Michaels, Kat Long, Lizzie Stanley, Blye Donovan, Bethany Monaco Smith, Elyse Kelly, and so many, many more.

Jeff, thank you for being the final nit-picky check to

make sure everything is perfect. Becoming a romance reader wasn't on your to-do list, but Jenni's grateful you did it anyway!

To all our friends and family, a big thank you because we love you, and your support is something we are eternally thankful to have.

ABOUT THE AUTHORS

AJ fell in love with Morgan's pen name, Gracie York, from *More than a Hero* and talked Jenni into bringing her books to life. Gracie York was born as a real-life author, and the two began co-writing. AJ is the plotter, organizer, and planner, so she writes all the bones of the story, then sends it back to Jenni. Then, when AJ is busy with her two kids, husband, and her house full of animals, Jenni goes through to add, edit, and tweak it. Which sometimes includes line editing her own sentences more than a few times to make it all just right. Then while AJ works on more bones, Jenni goes back to her four kids and day job as a paralegal in family law, writing real life unhappily ever afters all day. AJ and Jenni have not only become co-authors but great friends, and they can't wait to bring more of Gracie York's stories to life.

Made in the USA
Middletown, DE
15 May 2024

54395934R00102